# His Ladyship

## By Stevie Turner

Title:  His Ladyship
Copyright Stevie Turner © 2021
ISBN:  978-1838017163

## Dedication

For all those in the wrong body.

## Acknowledgements

Thanks to Phil Huston for the edits, and for providing many writing tips in his own inimitable style.

\*\*\*

Thanks to Teagan R. Geneviene for the book cover.

# Description

Norman Wicks is 57, overweight, and has diabetes. He is sick of his life. He has never left home, had a girlfriend, or held down any kind of job. The only friends he has are online, as he prefers to stay in the comfort zone of his bedroom. His devoted 92 year old mother Agnes waits on him hand and foot.

Norman has a secret he has kept hidden from the world for the majority of his life, but now he is desperate to bring it out into the open. He is terrified of how his family will react. However, for his own happiness and peace of mind, Norman must find a way to tell his mother and siblings exactly what they do not want to hear.

*HIS LADYSHIP* reached the finals and the Longlist of the 2021 Page Turner Awards.

# Table of Contents

# Table of Contents

## Chapter One – Norman
## October 1960

He knew he was different in some way to his brother Steven and sisters June and Ruth, but he did not know why or how. Norman Wicks, close to tears, sat at the breakfast table and turned the toy car over in his hands with great disappointment. His fourth birthday had not got off to a good start.

"I don't want it."

Steven, two years older, snatched it back with venom.

"That's the last time I give *you* anything for your birthday."

Their father, Hugh, reached across the table, took the car from Steven, and held it at arm's length in front of Norman.

"Don't be so ungrateful. Steven's bought you that out of his pocket money. He saved up for a long time. Take it and say *thank you*, like you *should* do when somebody buys you a present.

Norman's stomach gave a lurch of fright at the sight of his father's stern expression. He grabbed the hated toy Mini from his father's grasp.

"S-sorry Steven. Thank you."

He fervently hoped he might receive something he actually liked. So far there had been a regiment of toy soldiers from his mother, a train set from his father, and a football from his sisters. Norman didn't want any of them. Instead, he secretly coveted June's Tiny Tears dolly, who cried and wet its nappy. There was even a bottle of pretend milk that he had stuck in the dolly's mouth while June had not noticed, and when he'd upended the bottle the milk had disappeared just like magic. Ruth had a Tressy doll whose hair grew when he'd pressed its navel, amidst much shouting from his sister who had pushed him away as soon as he had touched it. Norman wanted his own Tiny Tears and doll's pram that he could wheel along the street just like June did. He hated football, and what use was a toy truck and tin soldiers?

Ruth, a haughty ten year old, gave him a hard stare.

"Perhaps he shouldn't have a birthday party then, if he's so rude."

"I *want* a party." Norman wiped away a stray tear with the back of his hand and kicked his legs under the table. "It's my *birthday*."

His mother finished a mouthful of food then put down her knife and fork.

"Of course you can have your party after school. Which friends did you invite?"

Norman knew his mother would always be on his side, and he basked in her warmth, safe from the wrath of his family. He sidled up to his mother and stuck out his tongue at Ruth.

"Amy and Gillian."

"Why no boys?" Steven crammed Weetabix into his mouth. "I wouldn't want girls at *my* party."

June, eight years old, laughed.

"He's a sissy. I've seen him in the infants' playground. He plays Mummies and Daddies with girls. He put some high heels on the other day."

Norman could not understand why it was wrong to play Mummies and Daddies with Amy and Gillian, or wear anything from the dressing up box. He disliked the boys at his nursery school, who were all too noisy and rushed about here and there and shouted for no real reason.

"If you've finished eating, Norman, then go and brush your teeth. Walk to nursery nicely with Ruth and June, and don't dawdle."

"Yes, Mum."

Norman got down from the table.

He knew the kitchen would soon be full of even bigger and noisier boys when Steven's friends arrived. Norman, happy to run up the stairs and wait until they had gone, gave his teeth a perfunctory clean. He then scuttled into the bedroom he shared with his brother until Steven had used the bathroom and gone off to school.

"Come on, we're waiting." June's head peered around the bedroom door. "Have you got your reading book?"

Norman grabbed his school bag and nodded.

9

They set off at a pace. Norman found it difficult to keep up with his sisters' long legs as they loped along.

"Hurry up," Ruth held out her hand, "or we'll miss the bell."

Norman entwined his fingers in hers. He had to run to keep up, which caused a slightly nauseous sensation as his breakfast sloshed about in his stomach.

Norman hated nursery school, and wished he did not have to go. He had no friends apart from Amy and Gillian, and Paul Coleman always took the mickey out of him when he played with dolls. Why was it wrong if he'd rather spend playtime with girls? Why *couldn't* he wear a dress and play Amy's mummy?

\*\*\*

Fists clenched at the sight of Amy, pretty in a pink frilly party frock and silver shoes, Norman muttered a greeting and then took a present from her outstretched hand. His mother gave him a nudge.

"What do you say?"

Norman looked at Amy and grimaced.

"Thank you."

Behind Amy and her mother stood Gillian Woodhouse, who lived just two doors away. When Amy's mother had departed, Gillian stepped forward with a carefully wrapped parcel in one hand.

"This is for you."

"Thanks." Norman took it and clenched his teeth.

His mother opened the front door wider.

"Come in girls, and you'll be able to play a bit before you have something to eat."

Norman stood in the hallway and tore at the wrapping paper with weary resignation; another Matchbox car from Amy, and a plastic airplane from Gillian. Tears of disappointment stung the back of his eyes.

When they looked through his toy box before tea he could tell that none of its contents had gained the girls' interest. However, when June grudgingly allowed Amy and Gillian to play with her dolls' house, Norman seized his chance and joined in, enjoying a rush of excitement when he was allowed to touch the usually forbidden figurines and tiny pieces of furniture. He spent a happy hour with his friends while they made up stories about the dolls' lives, and after his favourite tea of fish fingers, mash and spaghetti he knew it had been the best day he'd had in a long time, apart from the presents.

June guarded her treasured dolls' house with renewed fervour as soon as the girls departed. When Norman undressed for a bath, he piped up with a question that had been on his mind for some time.

"Can I have a dolls' house like June's?"

His mother laughed.

"What on earth for? You're a boy. Boys don't play with dolls' houses."

Norman's fist came down into the bath and splashed water over the carpet, much to his mother's annoyance. Life definitely was not *fair*.

"I want to be a *girl*!"

His mother, suddenly serious, lifted him up under the armpits and plonked him down in sweet smelling soapsuds.

"Believe me, Norman, you do not. Be thankful you're a boy. Boys get the best deal out of life."

Norman begged to differ, but decided not to argue. What was the point? He was a boy, and a boy he would have to stay.

\*\*\*

To his horror, the next day it was his turn to sit next to Paul Coleman. He knew it would be for just a single day, but one day was enough. He edged into his seat in silence, and pretended not to care about his close proximity to the boy whom he and all his classmates hated. Within minutes Paul's fist had made painful contact and hot breath hissed in his ear.

"Sissy…."

Norman rubbed his head and stared down at his pencil case, as their teacher shouted the words Norman wanted to hear.

"Paul Coleman… go and stand in the corner!"

"I'll get you at break." Paul muttered to Norman under his breath before standing up. "Just you wait."

Norman, temporarily free from the class bully, drew a picture of June's dolls' house in his diary. When he had been shown how to form the words to describe his drawing, Norman, with much difficulty, spent some time copying '*dolls' house*' underneath the teacher's neat writing. At

12

break time, terrified, he ran like the wind towards Ruth, who skipped with her friends in the junior's playground.

"You're not supposed to be here." Ruth let go of the skipping rope and took his hand. "Come on, I'll take you back to the Infants'."

"Paul Coleman's going to hit me again!" Norman wailed. "He said he'd get me at break."

"Oh, for God's sake, why don't you just hit him back?"

Norman ran alongside his sister to where Paul Coleman, alone as usual, kicked a ball with rather too much force at a classroom wall. Norman's bowels loosened as they approached. Ruth, a good foot taller, loomed over Paul with venom in her eyes.

"Touch my brother again, and I'll *kill* you."

The fear etched on the bully's face made Norman's day.

# Chapter Two – Hugh
## July 1969

Hugh Wicks tried to ignore the terrifying pain in his back, but the fact that he had just peed blood brought home to him the fact that the GP had been correct all along; he had advanced prostate cancer which was too far gone to do anything about. He had ignored the symptoms; he was doomed, and his premature death would be his own stupid fault for eschewing the radiotherapy offered, and surgery that might have made him impotent but somehow less of a man.

Agnes would need to know. She would be better at telling the children. *He was no good with the emotional stuff.* Hugh sank down onto the toilet seat and imagined how the kids would take the news of his impending demise. Ruth he knew would take it like the man she should have been. June would shout and wail, and Steven would keep his thoughts to himself. But Norman... there was something strange about Norman.

Time to stop being in denial. Hugh got to his feet with difficulty and rubbed his back. He would need to have a word with Agnes about their youngest son. However, he knew his wife doted on the boy and would not hear a word against him. Hugh remembered his own childhood spent mostly outside with other boys, and then Sandhurst and the

Army to rub off the raw edges. Norman had never shown any interest in sports, cars, bikes, the Military, or any other masculine pastimes. No friends came to the house, and he hardly ever went outside. He had tried to teach his son to stand up to bullies, but the boy was too timid. He had taken him to see Arsenal play, but Norman had no obvious interest in football that he could see. Instead he had shown much alarm at the roar from the spectators. Hugh compared him to Steven, and not for the first time wondered how on earth they could be brothers.

He knew his time on earth was coming to an end, and he was downright angry; angry at himself, and angry at the God he had prayed to every night. Why *him*? Why so soon? Why not let him live another few years so that he could sort Norman out for good? Time spent in the Army cadets would butch his youngest son up a bit. He needed to build up muscles and lose some of the puppy fat; the boy was just too sensitive for his own good.

\*\*\*

"It's worse than we thought, Aggie, I'm terminal. Doc says I've got about another six months."

His wife's face crumpled, and Hugh was at a loss for what to say next. He took Agnes's hand in his.

"There's enough money in the insurance policies, and there's also my Army pension. Ruth and June are out at work. You'll not starve."

"I can't believe this is happening." Agnes wiped her eyes with the back of one hand. "Have you told the children?"

"No." Hugh sighed. "Somehow I can't face it."

"I'll do it," Agnes sniffed, "but I don't know how Norman will take it. I don't think I'll tell him for a while."

"He needs bringing out of himself." Hugh patted his wife's shoulder. "Make sure he gets a paper round or a Saturday job. He's spending too much time alone in his room."

Agnes leaned against Hugh's chest.

"He's okay. He's just a normal teenage boy."

"He's not." Hugh shook his head. "He's totally different from Steven. I can't quite put my finger on it, but something isn't right with him."

Agnes sat up straighter. He looked her in the eyes. When she spoke he knew he was on a hiding to nothing.

"You're imagining things. He's fine. Leave him to me."

Hugh knew he would soon have to give up his job. What happened to Norman was now almost secondary to the agonising pain in his back.

## Chapter Three – Norman
## September 1971

Unlike Steven, nobody ever came to call for him to share the morning walk to school, and he was never picked for any sports teams. He had always been the embarrassed one who stood around on his own at break times while everybody else chatted in cliques and shut him out. Instead, the bullies were as merciless in the senior school as they had been in the juniors. He was different, an oddball, fat and cumbersome, and Stuart Binns and Denny McLeod took full advantage of his aversion to confrontations. And if that wasn't enough, with some alarm he realised that his voice had broken almost overnight. Hair he had never been aware of before had sprouted all over his body, a body which also contained a penis wildly out of control. He was horrified. He was turning into a man, and he could do nothing to stop it.

At the end of his tether, Norman decided that nobody would miss him if he bunked off school for good and amused himself at home instead. His father, the family's disciplinarian, had already been dead for over a year, but Norman knew he could wrap his mother around his little finger.

\*\*\*

"I don't want to go to school today." He bit into a cream cake. "They're all horrible to me and I can't stand it anymore."

He kept a downturned gaze, sniffed, and waited for his mother's reply.

"Shall I go and see your teacher?"

"Oh, no." Norman shook his head. "I'll just get beaten up if you do that. They were okay when Steven was there, but now he's left it's awful. I just don't want to go back at all."

"You've got exams next year. You won't pass if you don't go to school."

Norman shoved the last of the cake into his mouth.

"I don't care. Just let me stay at home Mum... *please*."

"What about another school? Shall I get on to the council and ask if you can be transferred?"

"No." Norman sighed. "It won't make any difference. It'll be the same wherever I go. People just don't seem to like me."

Out of the corner of his eye he saw his mother sidle around the breakfast bar and sit down next to him.

"You miss your dad, don't you?"

Norman squeezed out a couple of tears that ran down his cheeks.

"Every day. I still can't believe he's gone."

"He would have told you to stand up to them."

"There's too many." Norman sniffed. "It's no use."

18

To his surprise his mother gave him a hug.

"You're sixteen next year. Perhaps start to have a look around for work instead."

\*\*\*

Nobody came to the house to ask why he did not attend school. Norman soon ceased to worry that school inspectors might manhandle him, kicking and screaming, back to class. Amy and Gillian were now seniors in the girls' school, and he had no friends nor any opportunity to acquire new ones. Norman's kingdom remained his bedroom, and when Steven started work and shared a flat with two workmates, their bedroom became his and his alone. One by one June and Ruth married and moved out, and left their little brother to his own devices. His mother furnished his room with a new carpet, a double bed, a large TV, a radio, and a record and cassette player. Norman spent much time recording songs onto cassettes from the radio, interspersed with napping, reading and eating.

To please his mother he would walk to the main shopping centre on sunny days and look for work, but the result was always the same; he was not old enough and should still be at school. To pass the time before he returned home he would sit by the window in the Wimpy bar and make one hamburger last an hour. Girls paraded to and fro along the High Street, and Norman would watch their legs and wonder what it was like to have what they had under their skirts.

\*\*\*

By the time he *was* old enough he could not find any work that he considered suitable. He shied away from anything to do with engineering, building, trade apprenticeships and motor mechanics, and being in the world of the macho male. He envied women with their typing skills, and wondered why they always had the monopoly on office work. He yearned to learn shorthand and embark on a secretarial course, but he knew as usual that he would be the odd one out. He signed on for unemployment benefit and hoped for a miracle.

## Chapter Four – Norman
## 1976

His dole money came in every month without fail, and with no other financial demands he was able to buy the latest Betamax video player and up to date hi-fi system. A shop had opened in the High Street that rented out videos, and Norman enjoyed time to be able to watch several dubious films off the top shelf in private until his mother came home from work.

One sultry summer afternoon he knew the house would be his until at least half past three. Norman reached into the back of his wardrobe and pulled out a yellow sundress he had bought for 50 pence at a local jumble sale just the week before. He laid it on his bed and stared at it for some time. Finally he removed his jeans and tee shirt and pulled the dress on over his head.

The sight of himself in the mirror was less than satisfactory. Rolls of fat caused the sundress to bulge out around the waist area, and dark chest hair poked out instead of what should have been a smooth décolletage. Norman, disgusted, ripped off the dress, flung it back in the wardrobe, and then flopped face down upon the bed.

However, there was still an hour before his mother returned, and it was too hot to sleep. Norman got up from the bed and wandered into his mother's bedroom. Make-up lay strewn about the dressing table, and with a thumping heart he gazed at the lipsticks, eye shadows and mascara.

Unable to quell the urge any longer, he dabbed a finger in some blue eyeshadow and just like he had seen his mother do, he ran the one blue finger over his eyelids. He then picked up a lipstick and with shaky hands applied it to his mouth. Amazed at the transformation, he tossed his shoulder length hair from side to side like ladies did in the shampoo adverts on TV. He pouted, preened and stared at his reflection until the bedside carriage clock chimed three.

Alarmed, Norman returned all make-up to the correct places on his mother's dressing table, then ran into the bathroom and washed every guilty piece of evidence off his face. He hid the yellow sundress under his bed. Promptly at three thirty he heard a key turn in the lock.

"Hello Norman, I'm home!"

Norman came out from his room.

"Hi, Mum. Good day at work?"

"The kids were noisy because they don't like mince and mash, and the new recruit took ages to wash up. I had to help her. What have you been up to?"

"Oh, not much. I went to the Labour Exchange to see if there were any jobs I could do."

"Oh yes? And were there?"

"No." Norman shook his head. "But I'll keep an eye out."

"You do that. Surely you don't want to spend your whole life stuck in your bedroom?"

The chance to be idle, eat away the afternoon and to try on dresses and make-up compared to potential relentless ridicule at some dead end job appealed to Norman. He gave a thin smile to his mother.

"Of course not, but I'm only twenty. By this time next year I would have found a job. I'll get something, don't worry."

"Look at your brother. Steven's already on the career ladder at that insurance firm. June's a new mum, and Ruth's just got her nurse registration. You need to get out into the world, Norman, otherwise life will pass you by."

The same old lecture assailed his ears like a gramophone record whose needle had become stuck in one groove. Norman was sick of it.

"Yes, I know. Don't worry, Mum. I'll go back to the Labour Exchange again tomorrow."

"Make sure you do, son. Make sure you do."

\*\*\*

"You cannot carry on and claim unemployment benefit if you consistently refuse the vacancies we give you. You must take up this offer of employment otherwise we will stop your payments."

Norman regarded the smug bastard behind the desk of the Labour Exchange and wanted to smack him in the face.

"Okay, where do I have to go?"

"To the warehouse at the back of the Spendnsave supermarket in the High Street. You'll be helping to unload and store goods from the lorries. They will teach you how to drive a forklift. This is your last chance."

Norman could not think of anything worse, and was filled with an overpowering dread. He sighed.

"Okay. When do I start?"

"At nine o'clock on Monday morning."

"Do you have any work that's office based?"

"No. You're a strapping lad. Women work in the offices. Would you really want to work with a load of gossiping women?"

Norman shook his head and resisted a strong urge to answer in the affirmative.

\*\*\*

He knew he would hate the job the moment he stepped under the roll-up security door. One alpha male complete with tattooed muscles manoeuvred a forklift truck and unloaded boxes from a lorry parked out in the forecourt. A second alpha male lifted boxes of bananas off pallets and onto a conveyer belt, and shouted vulgarities at the first one, who gave back as good as he got. A third man, huge and hairy, talked and laughed out on the forecourt with the lorry driver.

"Hi I'm Norman."

The hairy one broke off his conversation and gave the new recruit a once-over.

"Yeah, I can see that. You look a right *Norman* to me."

Norman cringed to the depths of his being, then walked further into the warehouse. The man who lifted banana boxes with ease looked at him and snarled.

"Yeah?"

"Er... I'm Norman. I've started work here today."

"Good God." The man looked over at his colleague driving the forklift. "Look what we've got here!"

The forklift came closer and the driver leaned out the side.

"What is it?"

"It's a *Norman*. It's working with *us*."

"You've got to be joking." The forklift driver got out. "I reckon that's more like a Norma, don't you?"

Banana man nodded.

"Let's find out, shall we?"

To his horror, Norman suddenly found himself held in a vice-like grip by the two alpha males, while the third one and the lorry driver ran towards them and laughed.

"Initiation! Initiation! Get 'em off!"

"Leave me alone!" Norman struggled to free himself. "Stop it!"

"Stop it?" Banana Man laughed. "We all had to go through this on our first day, so why should *you* be any different? Welcome to the warehouse, mate."

Norman, terrified and disgusted, fought in vain as first his shoes and then his jeans and underpants were pulled off. Cool air blew around his genitals. He had never been naked in front of anybody in his entire adult life, and his embarrassment knew no bounds.

"I'll get the police on you!"

With a thump he landed on the ground and scrabbled around for his clothing. The men laughed. Forklift driver went back to work. Banana Man patted him on the back.

"Yeah, it's a *Norman*. Just had to make sure. Put the kettle on and make some coffee for a start. Two sugars in mine."

Norman, angrier than he had ever been in his life, pulled on his underpants in record time, then forcefully zipped up his jeans and shoved his feet into his shoes. He ran as fast as he could out of the warehouse to ribald laughter which emanated from somewhere behind him.

"We won't be seeing *him* again."

Norman could only agree. *If he could not work with women in an office, then dole money or no dole money, he would not work at all.*

# Chapter Five – Norman
# 1986

He found out that if he attended enough job interviews and acted on his worst behaviour, he could keep the vagaries of the Labour Exchange at bay and retain his dole money. Norman, certain that the nightmare of the warehouse would be forever fresh in his mind, bought himself a CB radio and retreated into the safety of his bedroom. With some trepidation he set it up, fixed an aerial to the outside wall, and switched to Channel 9 to try and make some contact, any contact, with the outside world.

"This is Hot Rod. Hot Rod. Anybody about?"

Over the white noise and brief snatches of other people's conversations came the sound of a distinctively female voice.

"Hi Hot Rod, this is Peachy. Can you hear me?"

His heart leapt at the sound of his new CB handle.

"I hear you, Peachy. Loud and clear. Whereabouts are you?"

"Switch to Channel Fifteen, Hot Rod. It's a clearer signal."

Excited, Norman tuned in.

"Peachy, this is Hot Rod."

"This is a better channel. Not so many people use it at the moment. I'm in sunny Addiscombe, Hot Rod."

"Where's that?"

"Near Croydon. How about you?"

"Fulham. Just as sunny today."

"So… do you work, Hot Rod?"

"In-between jobs at the moment."

"I'm a hairdresser."

"Great. Do you live with your parents?"

"No. I live over my shop. How about you?"

"I still live at home."

"No girl, Hot Rod?"

"Er… not at the moment."

"Fancy an eyeball?"

Norman, perplexed, wondered if he had heard right.

"A *what*?"

"An *eyeball*. Meet up. Do you want to? What about it?"

"Er…sure. I can get the train. What's your nearest station?"

"Elmer's End, Hot Rod. I'll wait for you at the station tomorrow. Eleven o'clock. I'll wear jeans and a yellow jacket. I'm always punctual, and I'd appreciate it if you could be the same."

"Sure." Norman knew he would be there half an hour early. "I won't be late."

\*\*\*

He could not believe a date had happened so soon. He took time over his appearance for his first meeting with a member of the opposite sex. He could tell his mother was curious, but he decided that she could stay that way. He was thirty years old, still a virgin, and it was about time he went out with a girl.

On investigation there were too many train changes. He decided it would be quicker and an easier option to take a taxi for the ten mile journey. He could afford it, and anyway, what else was there to spend his dole money on? Norman bought some Brut aftershave, washed his hair, and wished he were a few stones lighter.

"Why have you ordered a taxi, Norman?"

His mother didn't miss a trick. He likened her to an all-seeing eye and an all-hearing ear.

"I'm off out for an eyeball."

"A what?"

"An eyeball."

"What's the matter with your eyes?"

"Nothing."

\*\*\*

At ten to eleven Norman looked out of the taxi window as it approached Elmer's End station. A woman old enough to be his grandmother stood at the entrance in too-tight jeans and a bright yellow jacket, and peered in his direction. He dropped down in haste, and laid sideways on the seat.

"Sorry. Could you take me back to Fulham please? I've changed my mind."

"Whatever you want." The taxi driver replied with a shrug. "You're the one with the money."

\*\*\*

By the amount of abuse Peachy put out over various channels after his non-arrival, the writing was on the wall for Hot Rod. Norman worked to raise the pitch of his voice so that Lesley could emerge from the shadows. He could hardly wait to turn on the CB radio each morning, learn a bit more trucker slang, and morph into the girl he yearned to become. Lesley, bold, cheerful and outgoing (much to his surprise), had quite a number of followers after only a few weeks.

"Hi darlin'. Got your ears on?"

Norman recognized the throaty tones of Sid, the lewd lorry driver, and his heart sank in dismay.

"Hi Sid."

"I'm in London for a couple of days."

"That's nice."

"It'd be even nicer if I could meet up with *you*."

Norman wracked his brain.

"I've got an…um…broken leg at the moment. I'm confined to my bed."

"Even better. I could come and rub it better."

Norman recoiled in disgust.

"Er… my boyfriend might have something to say about that."

A lecherous chuckle came over the airwaves.

"Shame."

Another voice piped up; one he did not recognise.

"Yeah, shame. This is Steam Train, not Sid. I could have done a better job than *him*."

"We could have a threesome?" Sid volunteered with a laugh. "As long as Lesley's in the middle."

"Forty two." Steam Train roared in approval. "Forty two."

Norman sighed and wondered whether there were any CB radio users who were genuine and just wanted a chat with a woman without the ever-present sexual innuendo. It wasn't much to ask... *was it?*

Over time he became disillusioned; CB radio was no place for a woman. Norman revived Hot Rod after Peachy disappeared without trace, but when he spoke to other men as himself instead of Lesley it somehow just wasn't the same. He eventually took down the aerial and hoped Lesley's spirit lived on in the minds of faceless radio handles out there in the ether.

# Chapter Six - Norman
## 1990

"You ought to join a club. You would be able to make friends that way."

Norman bit back yet another tide of anger. If Ruth mentioned his lack of a social life just once more, then he would not be responsible for his actions. To make matters worse, his mother carried on the conversation as though he was not even in the room.

"He's not one to mix. He's quiet. You *know* what he's like. He's anti-social."

"I am *here*, you know." Norman shoveled a slice of chicken into his mouth "For your information I'm happy with my own company."

Ruth helped herself to some more roast potatoes.

"No you're not. You hardly say anything and you're downright miserable. So would *I* be if I sat in my room all day. Get a job for a start. You're perfectly capable of working. Why don't you? Why should *I* pay tax to keep the likes of *you*?"

"Leave him alone." Gordon gave Ruth a stare. "Just because *you* wouldn't like to sit in your room all day, that doesn't mean it's not right for everybody else in the whole wide world."

Norman nodded in agreement and tried to pretend it was commonplace for a man of almost 35 years of age to spend all day cooped up in his bedroom.

"Yeah, Ruth. Why don't you mind your own business? I *do* look for work… it's just that I haven't found anything suitable yet."

Ruth snorted.

"You obviously don't look hard enough."

June helped herself to some more gravy.

"Look, we've all come to visit Mum for the day. Let's see if we can get on for just a few hours, eh?"

"You can come to the pub with me, if you like." Steven reached to the next chair and gave Norman a pat on the back. "We can have a few pints when Hannah's not out at Pilates or Yoga and I don't have to babysit. We can even chuck in a game or two of Darts."

"I don't drink alcohol. I'm on Metformin, and the doctor doesn't advise it anyway. I've never played Darts, so I'd be useless at it."

Steven shrugged.

"Well, have an orange juice then and forget the darts."

"A night out with Norman." Ruth snorted. "I don't think I could stand the excitement."

June and Freddie giggled.

"I'm out of here." Norman stood up. "I've had enough. It was nice to know you all… *not*."

"*Now* look what you've done." Agnes glared at Ruth. "You've upset him."

Ruth shrugged.

"He's always upset. I'm sick of walking on eggshells around him. He's bloody *lazy*, that's what he is."

Norman stomped off to his room and slammed the door. None of his siblings, in-laws, or even his own mother knew why he *was* so downright miserable. It wasn't because he was desperate for a friend, although it would have been nice. No, the black cloud that hung over him was for an entirely different reason; one that he hated to admit to himself.

He wanted a girlfriend, but in a lesbian relationship. *Yes, that was the problem. He was a lesbian.* He could hardly admit it to himself, but yes, a lesbian he definitely was. He could imagine Ruth laughing herself into a heart attack at the thought of it.

Norman locked his bedroom door, then threw himself face down upon his bed. *Why was he so fucked up?*

He sobbed at the injustice of it all.

# Chapter Seven - Norman
## 2001

He was as big as a house. Norman hated himself, and especially his inability to lose any weight. *Life had indeed passed him by.* He was 45 years old, and had never secured a job, a girlfriend or even a male friend. Food was his lover. Every day was the same. He got up, took his diabetes tablet, ate breakfast that his mother cooked for him, and then sat in his bedroom and watched porn on his computer or slept, interspersed by lunch, dinner and many, many snacks.

"More bacon, Norman?"

Bacon and tomato sauce baps were a cure for the blues. Norman came out of his reverie with a start.

"Yes please."

He bit into another bap and wondered what his mother would say if she ever found out that he had yearned for years to become a woman. The secret bag of women's clothes and make-up under his bed had been there for a long time and could only ever be brought out when he was alone in the house. Norman chewed without tasting and wished he had never been born.

The porn had become a habit, and he was already hooked. All his life he had been ridiculed, teased, ignored, and rebuffed, and the porn gave him a little bit of pleasure.

However, would he be destined to spend the rest of his life in his bedroom? What had he ever done to displease the High and Mighty Creator so much? *Was there in fact such a person, like his father had stated?* Norman had his doubts.

He could not understand why his sisters and brother were straight as straight could be, but he himself had turned out such an aberration of nature. Weren't they all from the same mother and father? As he was the youngest, perhaps he had been conceived from older eggs and sperm? Maybe *that* had been the problem all along. Had he even *started* life on the back foot?

He stood up from the table, hating that his stomach was heavy and bloated.

"Thanks Mum."

He needed to sleep off his excesses. Norman, lethargic, waddled along the passageway to his room and flopped down upon his bed. A whole day stretched before him with not one thing to do except stare at porn and put a dress on whenever his mother decided to go out. Surely there was more to life? However, the older he became the more his confidence to change the situation ebbed away.

Norman shivered. *What would his family say if he ever came out as a woman? Would he ever be brave enough to live as Norma, the girl he should have been at birth?*

He could see no way out of his predicament. Norman closed his eyes and fell asleep.

\*\*\*

"Cup of tea for you."

Norman came to with a start and looked at the clock. Somehow two hours had gone by since breakfast, and he had forgotten to lock his bedroom door. He sat up and took the cup from his mother's hands, grateful that he had not gone to sleep with a nightdress on, as he had done on more than one desperate occasion.

"Ta."

"I'm off to my lunch club now. I've made you some sandwiches in the fridge. I'll be back about two o'clock."

"Okay Mum."

Three hours to pretend to be a woman. It was *something*, but it wasn't good enough. He needed to come out and tell the world, but was the world ready for the sight of Norma Jane Wicks in all her glory?

The tea had already cooled too much. Norman heaved himself off the bed and padded out to the kitchen. He was hungry again. Time to nuke the tea in the microwave and demolish a few chocolate digestives before he put on his make-up.

# Chapter Eight – Norman
## 2005

Girls were everywhere; on the bus, in the shops, and they pouted in front of him on his computer. Norman looked out of his bedroom window to see Chrissie, their next door neighbour, as she walked along the street. Norman, tormented with lust, swiveled back around on the chair towards his desk and put his head in his hands.

"Jesus Christ!"

Porn was no longer as exciting as it had been at the start. He had come to the conclusion that not one thing could take the place of a real live girl to embrace or even, if he was lucky, to make love to. An almost constant throb in his groin reminded him of the fucked-upness of his non-existent sex life.

*He was a lesbian. How the hell could he make love to a girl if he had a dick?*

He closed his eyes and thought about death and cancer until the sensation went away. He would be fifty the following year. *Fifty years of a wasted existence. He should have been at the top of the corporate ladder by now, with a girl to love and cherish, and a house of his own.*

Fat chance of that.

He imagined how it might be to end up dick-less, with breasts to die for and a smooth, slim, non-hirsute body.

The only place he did not have hair was on the top of his head, and that was where the stuff was *supposed* to be. His father's god played with him.

Norman closed his eyes and leaned back in his chair. *How the hell could he turn his life around with the duff hand he had been dealt? How could he escape the confines of his bedroom and live a normal life like his brother and sisters?*

If truth be told, he was not happy with his own company. He had lied to his family and indeed, had spent his whole life living one falsehood after another. He had even eaten himself into diabetes to try and dull the pain.

There was only one option; he would have to *come out* and face even more ridicule. But how? When? The whole scenario played over and over in his mind; the stares and the taunts, and himself the butt of a thousand jokes.

But then an idea struck him. *Why not wait until his elderly mother had died?* At least then he would not have to blurt out his oh-so-shameful secret to the person who loved him the most. At a pinch he could deal with June and Steven and maybe even Ruth if he took a deep breath, but to come out to Saint Agnes, as he knew Hannah usually called her, was something entirely different. *Yes, waiting was just what he would do.*

A wave of frustration tinged with slight relief washed over him; he did not have to shock his family right at that particular moment. His secret could wait. *He* would wait for however long it took. His mother must not know the innermost secrets of his heart; there were too many of them to count.

# Chapter Nine – Norman
## March 2014

"Fuck it!"

Norman gave the evil eye to a ladder which had appeared in the right leg of his brand new pair of nylon tights. With one smooth motion he yanked the tights down over his paunch, hopped from foot to foot to rip them off, and then flung them to the furthest corner of his bedroom just as his mother's bony knuckles rapped a sharp tattoo on the door.

"Norman… have you checked your sugar and taken your tablet?"

A stab of alarm brought him back to reality as the knob began to turn anti-clockwise. He now had to get to the door before all hell was let loose. Norman's left hand pulled his underpants further up around his waist, and as he ran towards the door he sweated and blasphemed at his forgetfulness to apply the bolt.

"Yes, Mum!" He panted, slamming the bolt home. "This morning."

"What?"

Norman wished for the thousandth time that his mother would turn on her hearing aid.

"This morning." He gasped. "I've done both. You don't need to worry."

"Good boy."

He could hear the old woman's squeaky-wheeled trolley making its usual excruciatingly slow progress as it trundled back along the carpet towards their front room. It was two o'clock, his mother had already brought him his usual cup of tea, and now two delicious hours stretched ahead of him while the old lady sat in her armchair for an afternoon rest. Norman's breaths returned to an even keel as he exhaled in relief and padded back to the mirror.

Draped seductively over a foam-padded hanger, his new olive green velvet dress with its flattering dropped waist oozed a kind of faded twenties' chic elegance. Excited, he fingered the soft material and then with some care removed the dress from its hanger and laid it on his bed next to a dark green bra and half-slip which had just arrived that morning to complete the ensemble. He picked up the bra, and his heart beat an excited tattoo in his ears.

Copious coarse hair on his abdomen caught in unfamiliar hooks and eyes. He freed the hated hirsuteness, pulled the bra up and around to the front, and gave a *tut* of annoyance as the boned contraption dug into the flesh under his nipples. He regarded himself in the mirror, poked a finger into the front of each pert cup, and grimaced as both deflated quicker than an undercooked soufflé. The elastic waist of the half-slip strained under pressure from his sizeable girth.

Norman shimmied over to where the laddered tights skulked in a corner. As he picked them up, the half-bitten nail of his middle finger caught in the nylon and tore it all over again.

"Bastard tights…"

He stuffed the tights down into the left cup of his bra, which to his surprise did an excellent job of filling out the dent. A pair of socks on the right hand side evened out a peculiar lopsidedness.

The size 26 dress slipped with ease over his head. It seemed a little tight around the middle, but it was the décolletage which caught his eye more. Black chest hair poked out above the low neck where an enticing vision of smooth, plump breasts should have been.

*What the hell was the matter with him? Why was he even doing this?* He wanted to scream. No matter what his reflection confirmed, inside he knew that Norma Jane Wicks was trying… no, *needed* to push past Norman John and get out. He lifted his arms skywards and looked up, an action which produced a small but definite rip in a side seam of the dress.

"Oh God!" Norman wailed. "Give us a break, will ya?"

It was time to eschew the easy option of doing nothing at all about his predicament. With some difficulty he removed the dress and bra, then flopped down upon the bed. *Life was too complicated.* His sisters and brother were in for a shock, to say nothing of what might happen to his 92 year old mother Agnes when Norma Jane appeared before her in full female regalia. Norman decided to give up the possibly lengthy wait until Agnes had departed for the celestial fields. His grandmother had lived until she was 103, and he definitely could *not* tarry for another decade as morbid obesity, diabetes and longevity did not go hand in hand. He closed his eyes and hoped with much fervour that he would not wake up.

\*\*\*

"Norman! Dinner time!"

The locked door rattled and brought him unwillingly out of his reverie.

"Okay…. Okay…" Norman rolled off the bed, threw on a pair of jeans and a tee shirt, and with one hand smoothed down the few sparse hairs either side of his bald pate where previously thick, dark hair once swung down to his shoulders. "I'll be there in a minute."

His mother was already seated at the table, her osteoporotic back protected by a swathe of cushions. He ignored her gimlet-eyed stare and looked down with distaste at the shepherd's pie and array of fresh vegetables in front of him.

"Why did you lock your door?"

"I didn't have any clothes on, Mum."

"What?" Agnes pushed a few peas around her plate. "Why not?"

He knew the stubborn old woman would not be put off. Norman shoveled a forkful of mash into his mouth and wracked his brains for a suitable reason for being naked in the middle of the afternoon. He decided to ignore her first question, as she often replied *what* to anything he said out of habit. Her second question was somewhat trickier to answer. Norman chewed mechanically and considered whether to let the cat out of the bag and tell his mother what he had really been up to.

"I had a shower and then fell asleep."

"Oh."

He hated himself because once again he had put off the evil moment for yet another day, but rationalised there was a proper time and place for everything. He was not brave enough to cope with a mother who might choke on her dinner. His siblings needed to be present to help manage the inevitable crisis caused by his *coming-out*. He would definitely 'emerge' in the very near future, because currently he just *existed*. His life had to change, or the rest of it would not be worth living at all.

# Chapter Ten – Agnes

Agnes picked up her own and Norman's dirty plates and cutlery with difficulty, and placed them on the top shelf of her walker. Over the past year it had become harder to grip anything, or to balance without a mobility aid such as her redundant hostess trolley, re-purposed now to a walker with shelves. She had not been a hostess for years, and who the hell ever came to see them anyway apart from Ruth and Gordon, June, and Steve (she had long ago accepted that Hannah would never accompany him)?

As Agnes stumbled along at a snail's pace towards the kitchen sink she wondered how much longer she could cope without any kind of domestic help, because the only person who could have made the task of washing the dishes easier had once again vanished into his bedroom to lie on his bed and be waited on like Lord Muck.

Agnes positioned the walker to the right side of her with one hand, and with the other pulled a high stool up to the sink and sat down upon it with a grateful sigh. Her skinny arms transferred the encrusted pie dish, plates, knives and forks into a washing-up bowl. She added some detergent, then ran the hot water. No longer was she able to bend down and put all the dishes away in the cupboard;

she mused on how the rinsed crockery would need to stay on the draining board.

She transferred the first plate to the rack with more force than necessary, aggrieved at her youngest son's lack of support. She had not argued with him during his adolescence about his unwavering ability to dodge chores, even though his reluctance to help around the house was already much to the fore by the age of thirteen.

Agnes recalled her own brother John, long since passed, his enviable ability to escape any domestic issues as a young man, and their mother's calm acceptance that men were exempt from any household duties. However, with no wife to train him, Norman had failed to grow out of a similar behaviour to John's, sadly perfected over a 40 year period and which unfortunately had now become embedded in his psyche. Had it been *her* fault all along why her son was so selfish? Had she done too much for him?

Even washing up a few plates now was a struggle, and Agnes was exhausted. Soon Norman would need a supper of some sort, and another cup of tea. She wiped her hands on a piece of kitchen paper and managed to grip the trolley once more. She concentrated on rising to her feet, but looked forward to another little sit-down and the chance for a nap. Life in extreme old age was hard; harder than it had ever been before.

\*\*\*

The telephone brought her to consciousness with its shrill, incessant ring. Six o'clock and time for the first of her three other offspring to report in with what she had long ago deduced were duty calls to bring her up to date with every single banal event of their day. Certain her daughters always spoke in soft voices just to spite her, Agnes placed the receiver next to her left ear, and made sure the volume was turned up to its highest level.

"Hello!"

"You don't have to shout, Mum."

Her daughter sounded edgy and irritable. Perhaps Ruth and Gordon had argued yet again, or maybe it was the same row that had been left to smoulder on from the week before.

"What?"

"Don't shout!"

"I'm not." Agnes strained to hear Ruth's words. "Are you all packed up now?"

"Yes, we're off early in the morning. We can't wait to get to Saint Lucia and get a bit of sunshine."

"You've got a bad line?" Agnes transferred the phone to her other ear. "What did you say?"

"Mum... put your bloody hearing aid in!"

Agnes held the phone slightly away from her face until her daughter had finished shouting like the old fishwife she had become.

"*You* wear one and then you'll know why they're all useless. They amplify *everything*, not just your voice."

"*Whatever.*" Ruth replied with venom. "I'm sure you'll hear much better if you just give it a try. Anyway, what have you been up to today?"

Agnes sighed.

*As if Ruth cared a jot... tidied the beds, gave Norman his tablet, dusted with one hand as the other had to hold onto the trolley, made lunch, slept, cooked dinner, and tried to sleep again until the bloody phone rang.*

"Oh, the usual. Not much..."

"When we get back we'll come down and take you out for a meal."

Agnes recognized her daughter's feigned enthusiasm and pulled a face.

"You go off. I'm fine. Norman's fine. Have a good holiday."

She ended the call and waited for the next intrusion, which came soon enough and coincided with Norman's voice as he shouted from his room for his usual brew. She looked down at the number display.

"Hello Steven."

"Hey Mum, how's it going?"

His deep, resonant voice was always easier to hear.

"It's gone, darling."

His throaty chuckle lifted her mood somewhat.

"Mum, I can hear that lazy git in the background. Tell him to get off his fat, lazy arse and fetch his own cup of tea."

"Oh, it's no trouble." Agnes lied. "I don't mind."

49

"If I was there I'd kick his arse all the way to the kettle."

*But you're not here, are you?* Agnes bit back the tart reply.

"He's not well, Steven."

She was sure she had heard a snort of impatience at the other end.

"It's all put on, Mum. He lies on his bed all day and barks out orders. There's nothing wrong with him apart from the fact that he's too fat. I'll have a word in his ear if you like. There are thousands of people who live with diabetes. They go to work, drive cars, and have their own places. You know that if Dad were still alive he'd have told him to get a job years ago."

"No need. We're fine, honestly."

"I'll be down in a fortnight, anyway. It's about time Norm started pulling his weight."

*And what a weight!*

"I've got to put the kettle on, now. Speak to you soon. Love you."

She tried to ignore the pregnant pause.

"Bye Mum."

Agnes rocked herself up out of the armchair and held on to the trolley for dear life. She hoped her shrill, raspy voice would carry through the bedroom door.

"Norman…I'll put the kettle on!"

\*\*\*

She waited for the water to boil and had a brief flashback to Hugh, proud military man to the end, and remembered his intolerance of any kind to what he considered 'slacking' in his children. Her older three had all secured newspaper rounds at fourteen, and enjoyed the money they earned from their work. Norman had lost his father at the same age, when a boy should have had his dad around to encourage the work ethic that had been such a success with the others. She knew she had mollycoddled her son at the time of her husband's death; Norman would not mix with his peers, and did not want to go out. One thing had led to another. Food had replaced his father's guidance and she knew she had let her son get away with too much for 43 years, especially with regards to his lack of employment. He'd had too easy a life, and now she had to pay for her mistakes.

The phone rang again just as she poured hot water into a teapot. Agnes sighed. Whoever it was would have to wait; Norman had to come first. By the time she delivered the tea, she had counted 72 rings. She plodded back towards the phone, but the ringing stopped as she reached out to lift the receiver. She muttered a curse under her breath; now she would have to stand there and wait for the bloody thing to ring again.

# Chapter Eleven - June

"Why doesn't the stupid man ever answer his mobile?"

June exhaled with some force then tried her mother's landline once again. To her surprise the phone was answered almost straight away.

"Hello? Yes?"

The familiar quivery voice caused her to breathe a sigh of relief. *Another potential dash to the hospital averted...*

"I've been ringing for ages. I tried Norman's phone as well, but *he* didn't answer either."

"What?"

"Where have you been?" June bellowed down the line. "I've been worried about you!"

"I haven't been anywhere. I've just made Norman a cup of tea."

"Tell him to answer his phone sometimes, Mum. Why does he have a mobile if he never speaks to anyone?"

"Well, it's *me* who tends to pick up the phone, and so I expect he leaves it. Nobody ever rings for him anyway."

*That's right... defend him again, the peculiar bloke.*

"Yeah, but you don't have access to his mobile, do you?"

"What?"

*Yeah, yeah, pretend you haven't heard...*

"His mobile…you don't answer his mobile!"

"Of course I don't."

Her mother sounded affronted. June took a deep breath.

"How are you, anyway?"

"What? I'm fine." Agnes replied. "Don't you worry about *me*. Is Andrew enjoying University?"

"I'm sure he is." June chuckled. "He hasn't been in touch, and so I take that as good news. He's found a girl up there, and I think he's discovered what it's all about. By the way, does Norman help you to take the rubbish out now?"

"I can manage it."

June sighed.

"I'll have to have a word with him. We don't want you to fall over on the path again and bash your head on the concrete. You could have killed yourself."

"I'll be more careful next time."

"Put him on." June's voice rose a couple of semitones. "This just isn't good enough. He doesn't lift a finger to help you, and it's about time he did!"

She knew the response even before the words had left her mother's mouth.

"I can't. He was asleep when I took his tea in."

June swallowed her anger and took a deep breath.

"Go and wake him up then. He shouldn't be asleep at this time of day. His body rhythms must have all gone to pot!"

"Oh… he's tired. Let him be. He's not well."

Was she brave enough to call her mother a liar? June squeezed her eyes shut and counted to ten.

"Not well? My arse! Tell him to phone me when he wakes up."

"I will."

"I'll be down at the weekend, and so if he hasn't phoned me by then I'll barge into his room and tell him what's what."

"What?"

"What's *what*, that's what.*"* June emphasised once more. "He needs to be sorted out, for sure."

Why did telephone calls to her mother always cause her blood pressure to rise? In the background she could hear the *arsehole's* plaintive but demanding whine.

"He's woken up, Mum. I can hear him. Take the phone to him. Go on…I'll wait."

June drummed the fingers of her right hand on one side of her chair, irritated at the painfully slow squeak of the trolley in her left ear, and wondered how much the phone call would eventually cost. After what seemed like an eternity she heard her mother clear her throat.

"June?"

"Yes, I'm still here."

"He says he's too busy to speak to you."

June briefly closed her eyes and counted to ten.

"Busy doing *what*? Don't worry, I'll be there on Saturday and I'll wait all bloody day until he *does* speak to me."

"Leave it. You know you'll only cause trouble."

June emitted a wry laugh.

"Trouble's my middle name. It's not right. You shouldn't run around after him at your age. *You* should take it easy, and *he* should be the one who waits on *you*."

"He gives me a reason to get up in the morning."

June took a few calming breaths and gave up.

"See you on Saturday, Mum."

## Chapter Twelve – Norma

He could hear June's voice in the front room as she struggled to permeate the old lady's eardrums. Norman checked his make-up in the mirror, added a bit more lipstick and mascara, and then with great care pulled a pair of fishnet tights up over his large thighs then stepped into a bespoke leather skirt that had cost him a sizeable chunk of one whole month's benefit payment. His tee shirt sparkled with sequins and clung in all the wrong places and his bra didn't quite give him the shape he wanted, but the transformation to Norma only encouraged an increasing urge to spend the remainder of his life as a woman.

Only one problem remained; well ... three to be precise. Norman gazed with contempt upon the male pattern baldness that had left him with copious hair on both sides of his head but just a small amount on the top. Furthermore, to make matters worse, despite having shaved that morning a five o'clock shadow had already peeped out from under his foundation. The third problem was how to rid himself of his penis, which disgusted him every time he looked at it.

Nevertheless, *it was now or never or not at all.* Norman made a mental note to check out a selection of wigs on the Internet, and then with his heart threatening to jump out of his chest he unlocked his bedroom door and with trepidation ventured into the passageway. He hesitated for a brief moment at the door to the front room, looked down and pulled out a dent in the left cup of his bra, and then sallied forth with false bravado.

The expression of disgust upon their faces would be forever seared in the forefront of his memory. His sister broke off mid-sentence and jumped up in undisguised horror, while the old lady, mouth agape with shock, sat forward in her armchair and stared at his legs. Norman stood his ground.

"What the *fuck*, Norman!" June walked towards him. "What the hell have you done to yourself? Stop it for God's sake! Have you taken leave of your senses?"

He swallowed what seemed like a pebble in the back of his throat and carried on.

"No, this is *me*. Norman's gone, and I shall be *Norma* from this moment on. For your information I've always been Norma inside, but now it's time to ditch the easy option and try to do something about it."

She hated her croaky, dark brown voice. She took a deep breath and then waited in silence. Her mother's head shook from side to side in oscillating negativity.

"You look ridiculous!"

"More like a drag queen." June put one hand to her mouth to stifle a giggle. "Sorry to laugh, but have you seen yourself in the mirror? You look like Freddie Mercury in that video... hoovering when he wanted to break free."

Norma knew there was no going back.

"I shall order a wig and go the whole hog... you know... have the op. "

"Norman, stop it." Agnes tried to lever herself out of the soft armchair. "This isn't funny anymore!"

June threw back her head and roared.

"It bloody well is! It's the Rocky Horror Show all over again! Whatever's Steve going to say? He won't believe this!"

Tears flooded Norma's eyes. She turned on her heel and ran back to the safety of her bedroom and a locked door between herself and the rest of the world. In her room she could be whoever she wanted to be without ridicule. She took a moment to compose herself, then wiped black tracks of mascara from her cheeks. Her sister's reaction had made her even more determined to reinvent herself and rise like a glorious phoenix from the ashes of Norman John Wicks' damaged and ugly body.

\*\*\*

She ignored the constant buzz of her mobile and re-applied her mascara. She was hungry and needed a drink. Three hours had now passed by since she'd 'come out'. She'd had a little nap and was now much calmer and more in control of her emotions.

Beyond the safety of the bedroom door she could hear June and now Steve in heated conversation. Steve had obviously been summoned to bring her to her senses, and knowing her brother as well as she did, he was not likely to leave until the situation had been resolved. Well, did she have a surprise for *him!*

The firm rap on her door caused her to jump in alarm.

"Norman! Open the bloody door!"

Norma stood up and crept towards the door.

"Didn't June tell you? I'm Norma now. Unless you address me as Norma, then I'll stay in here."

More heated whispers outside. Norma, one hand on the doorknob, tried to quell her breathing to a slower rate.

"*Norma!* Open the fucking door or I'm going to kick it in!"

Her fingers trembled. Norma turned the key and to her horror came eye to eye with Steve's crimson visage.

"What are you playing at? You've upset Mum! She doesn't know whether to laugh or cry. Are you drunk? Have you seen what you look like? Put your proper clothes back on!"

Norma stepped back in alarm from her brother.

"These *are* my proper clothes. I'm a woman now."

"No." Steve shook his head and sighed with much weariness. "You're a bloke who happens to be wearing a skirt and fishnet tights. Go out looking like that and some skinhead will beat you up for sure."

"I'm seventeen stone. He'll have a bit of a job."

"Yeah, you've got muscles like a bloke, because let's face it, you *are* a bloke." Steve pointed one finger. "You need a check-up from the neck-up, mate. Norman, nobody could ever take you for a woman. Christ almighty, look at the bloody size of you. What bloke is ever going to fancy *you*?"

Norma decided to bury all her bad news at the same time.

"I'm a lesbian. I only fancy girls."

June pushed past Steve and poked Norma in the chest.

"Because you're a *man*. You fancy girls because you're a *man*! Most men do, didn't you know that?"

"Yes." Norma hated how her voice wobbled. "But I'm not a man, I'm a woman!"

Steve regarded Norma with a trace of menace.

"Man *or* woman, you'd better get your arse off that bed and take the rubbish out when it's needed. If I get to hear that Mum's struggled out there with her stick in one hand and a sack in the other and has fallen over again, it'll be *me* who beats you up. The poor old girl is over ninety and you've never lifted a finger to help her. She can't do much now, and as *you* live here as well, then you'll *have* to do more. I don't care if you're gay, lesbian, bi, trans, or a bloody Red Indian chief, it's time you pulled your weight around here."

"Talking about weight." June interjected. "Try and lose some. You're almost as wide as the doorway. You'll feel more energetic if you eat healthily and don't weigh so much, take my word for it. Your diabetes might even get better."

Norma looked from one to the other of her siblings in disgust, and then slammed the door in their faces and drove the bolt home so that she could cry another river in private.

"That's it...shut yourself away again!" Steve roared through the partition. "You won't solve anything if you bury your head in the sand!"

Norma flung herself face down upon the bed and put her hands over her ears.

## Chapter Thirteen - Ruth

"Missy, I can braid your hair."

Ruth opened her eyes and frowned at a large woman who stepped under her parasol and held out a tray of necklaces and bracelets. This was the third interruption in twenty minutes, and now the woman had the cheek to enter her personal space. Ruth had had enough.

"I don't want my hair braided, thanks."

"How about a necklace to take home? Made right here in Castries. Ten dollars each."

Ruth regarded the woman with disgust and gave her what she hoped was her best frigid gaze. She had seen the same tat down the Camden Road market at probably a fraction of the price. Did she think all tourists were stupid?

"I'll tell you the same thing as I told the previous two that came round not even half an hour ago... I don't want my hair braided and I don't want whatever you're selling."

The woman sucked her teeth and moved away. Ruth turned her head to the right, where Gordon still lay asleep on one of the resort's uncomfortable sunbeds. She checked the position of the sun, then sat up and moved the parasol to give them both the maximum shade. She winced slightly as she massaged her lower back, and decided it was better to sit up straighter.

"I'm surprised you didn't tell her to piss off."

Ruth looked at Gordon in surprise.

"I thought you were asleep."

"Yeah, I was, but your voice woke me up."

She gazed somewhat enviously at her 63 year old husband, who still had only very few streaks of grey in amongst thick dark hair. Her own brown locks had turned silver back in 2002.

*Bastard!*

The warm sea shimmered blue, not one cloud spoiled the azure sky, and to all extents and purposes she should be content with her lot. However, Ruth knew she shared a parasol in paradise with entirely the wrong person. Her whole adult existence had seemingly been wasted. Life sucked, and not for the first time she envied her younger sister, now divorced. June had shed the ghost of Freddie like an old skin, and was quite content Internet dating and spending half of Freddie's not inconsiderable income.

"Are you going to sleep *all* day?"

She knew he hated the petulant tone in her voice, but she couldn't help it. Ruth swatted a fly, then tore off her sunhat to let a sudden breeze cool her forehead.

"I might. Why? What else do you want to do? I expect passionate sex is off the menu, and so perhaps we can play cards all afternoon?"

Gordon's biting sarcasm was fuel to the fire. Ruth gave a snort of annoyance, then heaved herself over to her front and turned her head away.

"Oh...go back to sleep."

Down in the depths of her beach bag she heard a short buzz. Too lazy in the heat to sit up, she hung one arm over the side of her sun lounger and fished about in her bag until she had located her mobile phone. When she saw a notification she raised herself up on one elbow and looked at the display screen.

"I've got a message from June."

Gordon remained silent. Ruth tapped on the message, then turned to look at her husband in confusion.

"What the *hell's* she taking?"

"Eh?" Gordon turned towards her and frowned. "What are you going on about?"

Ruth sat up straight and checked the message once again.

"She says Norman's now Norma, and that he's a lesbian."

"Bloody hell." Gordon spluttered with laughter. "She must have been on that sherry again."

"She does come out with the strangest things when she's drunk." Ruth sighed and sent a laughing emoji. "How can he be a lesbian? He's a bloke!"

"What about if she's serious?" Gordon put his hands behind his head and stretched out his legs. "Have you thought of that? Let's face it… he always *was* a bit strange."

Ruth stared at her phone.

"I'll call her, but not for long, in case it's expensive."

She tapped in her sister's contact details and let the phone ring several times before she ended the call.

"She's probably asleep. Three sheets to the wind I'll bet."

"Lucky old June." Gordon closed his eyes. "I bet *I'd* get a bollocking if I did the same."

Ruth ignored the remark and waved away a young man who carried a box laden with melon quarters.

"No thanks."

"Lovely melon. I give you nice price, my friend."

"Look … I said *no*. Okay?" Ruth sighed to emphasise her point. "Take your melons and shove them where the sun doesn't shine."

She flopped backwards onto the sunbed as Gordon let out a long, throaty chuckle at the man's retreat.

"You haven't lost your touch. The poor sod couldn't get away fast enough."

"Well…what do these people expect?" It's really cheeky of them to keep on annoying us like this." She swatted a passing wasp with her book then pointed a finger towards the far end of the beach. "See that hut? That's where they all come from. Every ten minutes one of them comes out with another tray of stuff to sell. I'm sick of it."

The phone cut short her diatribe. Ruth peered at the display screen.

"Ah, it's June." She pressed 'Accept'. "Hi. Have you been drinking?

"No I bleedin' well haven't!"

"So why did you say Norman's a lesbian?"

"Because he is." June's laughter tinkled down the line. "He's come out and announced it. You ought to have seen him in full drag and make-up. It was bloody scary!"

"Blimey." Ruth, mouth open in surprise, looked over at Gordon. "Straight up? You're not kidding?"

"Ask him yourself, or should I say *her*self. I don't know *what* he is anymore."

Ruth chuckled.

"I can't just now, 'cos I'm in Saint Lucia."

"Ooh, I forgot … this will cost me a fortune. 'Bye!"

The line went dead. Ruth put the phone back in her beach bag and then turned to Gordon, somewhat mystified.

"It's true. My brother is a *lesbian*. June says he's scary. Poor Mum. What the hell are we going to do about it?"

"Not a lot." Gordon yawned. "I think I'll go back to sleep. I suggest you do the same."

"He never *was* very masculine, and always preferred playing with my dolls. I wonder what caused him to come out at *his* time of life?"

She looked across at Gordon, whose breaths already came deep and even. Ruth let out a deep breath, then settled herself more comfortably on the sunbed. She closed her eyes, then frowned at the sudden blocking of sunshine.

"Pretty necklace, Missy?"

## Chapter Fourteen – Norma

She dressed as conservatively as she could; a long black skirt, a polo-neck jumper, and some new sandals that she'd had to order from a special website to fit her size 11 feet. Norma looked down with some satisfaction at two symmetrical bumps under her jumper, and marveled how the bra fillers had performed a much better job than two pairs of old socks. She finished painting her nails and then waved her hands around in the air to dry the varnish. She combed her new wig and revelled in silky ginger strands of hair that touched her shoulders.

It was time to venture out for the first time as a woman. With fingers that trembled she dialled the number of a local taxi service.

"AB Taxis. Can I help you?"

"Hello." Norma raised her voice to a higher pitch. "I'd like to book a return trip to my GP surgery please."

"Okay." A gruff voice replied. "What time is your appointment?"

"Eleven o'clock. My address is thirty six Crozier Road, Fulham, just around the corner from you."

"Yeah, I know the road. Where are you going to?"

"The Pinto GP Practice in Sala Road."

"A taxi will pick you up at half past ten."

"Thank you."

It was a strain to keep her voice pitched so high. Norma ended the call and looked at her watch; another hour to wait. She added two twenty pound notes from a drawer in her desk to her purse, and then pulled a jaunty hat down over her wig to keep it in place. A tote bag swung over one shoulder completed the ensemble. She unlocked her bedroom door and sashayed forth, and as she walked along the passage to the front room she enjoyed how the skirt felt as it swished around her ankles.

Her mother, chin on chest, had fallen asleep in the armchair. Norma plonked herself down in the chair opposite, and drummed her fingers on the arm rest as she waited for the old lady to rouse from her slumber. Presently there was a loud snort, and then her mother's head shot up in alarm.

"Wha…?"

"I'm going out in a minute, Mum." Norma looked at her watch and shouted louder. "I've booked a taxi to go to the doctor's."

"What?" Agnes coughed. "Why?"

"As you know I've changed to a woman now, but there's one thing that's still male and I want to get rid of it."

"You must be stark, staring mad." Agnes regarded Norma with contempt. "It's too late for me to even think of you as a woman. I've brought you up as a boy for almost sixty years, and that's what you are."

It was hopeless to argue with somebody so fixated in their own self-righteous beliefs. Norma stood up, gathered the folds of her skirt together, and made for the door.

"See you soon. I shall go outside and wait for the taxi."
***

She looked straight ahead at the receptionist and tried to ignore the many pairs of eyes focused upon her. She hated to give out any information when so many people were in her space but pretended not to listen.

"Norman Wicks to see Doctor Lewis. For your information I'd like to be known as Norma from now on. Please change my name on your notes."

The receptionist gave a quick double take.

"Have you changed your name by deed poll?"

"Er… no." Norma replied. "But I *will* do."

"When it's official, *then* we can change it."

Norma gave a sigh of irritation, but decided she had caused enough of a sensation already. She kept her eyes fixed on the floor and took a corner seat, aware of a snigger from a teenage girl who sat nearby with her mother. Flustered, Norma pulled her phone out of her bag, mentally punched the young girl's lights out, and pressed any button to look as though she had something to do.
***

"Mister Wicks, the doctor is free now."

Relieved at such a short wait, Norma jumped up and followed a nurse to the doctor's surgery, who as far as she could tell tried without success to pretend that a man dressed as a woman complete with size 11 sandals and painted toenails was an everyday occurrence.

"Er... Mister...Miss...Wicks... do sit down."

"Hello Doctor Lewis." Norma replied with more bonhomie than she felt as she took a chair. "It's Norma now so I'm a Ms, and that's what I've come to see you about."

"Not the diabetes?" The doctor appeared perplexed. "Do you still take your Metformin tablets and attend your appointments at the Community Glaucoma Clinic?"

"Yes, and yes." Norman nodded. "The diabetes is not what I'm here for, although if you could write me a repeat prescription it'll save you having to deliver them. Actually..." Norma's pulse quickened. "...I- I want a sex change. I've always been a woman in my head, and now I want to live like one before it's too late."

She pretended not to notice the doctor's unsuccessful attempt to hide his shock. He held up one hand.

"I'm afraid I'll have to stop you there. You will need to see another practice doctor, as gender reassignment surgery goes against my Christian principles, and about your other enquiry - we only issue repeat prescriptions once a month."

Irate, Norma got to her feet.

"God gave me the wrong body. It's not my bloody fault, it's His!"

Dean Lewis rose to his full height of six foot four inches and kept his voice even.

"Calm down Mister Wicks. I'll go and see if one of the other doctors are free."

"It's *Ms*, I just told you." Norma sniffed. "I don't want to be a Mister anymore. I'm a woman in my head. I've always been a woman, but God gave me a man's body. Perhaps he'd had an off day."

She saw how quickly the doctor averted his eyes at her words, then skirted around her and was out of the door in a trice.

"Please wait. I will return shortly."

She sat back on the chair and stared with some menace at the retreating back. On his return she noticed how the doctor left the door ajar and did not fully enter the room.

"Please pop along to room number eight. Doctor Freestone will see you now. He's new at the practice, and is still building up his list."

"Cheers." Norma got to her feet. "Sorry that I shouted."

"That's okay, just head on down the corridor."

Norma gathered her possessions, nervous to meet a new clinician whom she did not know. She gave a gentle tap on the door of room 8.

"Come in."

Isaac Freestone swiveled around in his chair.

"Er… Doctor Lewis sent me along. I'm Norman Wicks, although from here on in I want to be called Norma. Did he explain?"

"Yes." Doctor Freestone nodded. "Come and sit down. I gather you would like gender reassignment surgery?"

"That's right." Norma flopped into a chair and stared at the doctor. "I want to live as a woman."

Doctor Freestone tapped away at his computer.

"The surgery would happen only after you've lived as a woman for at least a year, possibly two. I would need to refer you to the NHS True Life Gender Dysphoria Clinic in Fulham, where first off they would offer you counselling and then if you like they can start you on cross-sex hormone therapy."

"Let's do it." Norma confirmed with a nod. "I'm ready. I've been ready for fifty seven years."

"One thing though…" The doctor waggled one finger. "They will not be able to change your height, the width of your shoulders, your facial features or your basic DNA. Your DNA will remain male, and that can never be altered. Further surgery in the private sector will be necessary for facial feminisation surgery. There is also private surgery available in some countries in order to change leg length, but it is expensive and painful."

"I gathered that." Norma nodded. "but I look forward to receiving an appointment for the NHS clinic."

"It might take a few weeks." Doctor Freestone got to his feet and held out his right hand. "In the meantime perhaps get used to dressing as a woman and try to get out and about more."

"Thank you." Norma stood up and shook the doctor's hand. "Thank you very much."

"It's not an easy road that you plan to go down. I hope you realise that."

"Of course, but I'm determined to change before it's too late."

She followed the doctor to the door of the surgery, who ushered her out into the corridor.

"Good luck to you."

Norma smiled.

"I've wasted so much time, and I can't afford to wait any longer. It's great that somebody has actually listened to me."

# Chapter Fifteen - Norma

She found the True Life Clinic tucked away in a side alley off the Fulham High Street. Norma, mouth dry and slightly nauseous, strode through the clinic's main door with rather more confidence than she felt.

"Good morning. Can I help you?"

The receptionist, blonde, pretty and petite, caused Norma to wonder whether she should try and reach for the moon instead. She looked down at her huge feet and tried to block out the vision of loveliness in front of her

"Hi. I have an appointment with Doctor Bryant. The name is Norma Wicks."

"Hello Norma." The receptionist indicated with one exquisitely manicured hand towards an empty waiting area. "You're the first one in today. If you take a seat over there, then Doctor Bryant will call you in very soon."

"Thank you."

Heart performing somersaults, Norma took a magazine from the central table and sank down into an armchair with some relief, but could not concentrate on reading even one article. When a diminutive middle-aged lady in a white coat came out to greet her, Norma, lost in thought, leapt up like a startled fawn.

"Norma Wicks?"

"That's me." Norma stretched out her right hand. "Pleased to meet you."

The hand that grasped hers was warm and soft.

"I'm Doctor Bryant. Please follow me and we can have a little chat."

Relieved to see a jug of water and two glasses on the desk between them, Norma filled a glass straight away.

"Sorry, I'm really dry...nerves I suppose."

"Don't worry, I completely understand." Doctor Bryant sat down. "Have a seat. It's a big step you've made today. Most people are nervous when they first come here."

"I want it all taken away." Norma sighed. "I want to be a woman."

Doctor Bryant logged into her computer.

"You realise this means that you will need to have extensive male to female gender reassignment surgery and lifelong hormone treatment with oestrogen, progesterone and also a testosterone blocker."

"*Yes.*" Norma nodded with some enthusiasm. "When?"

"After counselling." Doctor Bryant looked up from the screen and chuckled. "We can't just rush into something like this. You will be seen for a few sessions of counselling by our psychologist and given information and advice, and then if you still want to go through with surgery you will be added to the waiting list. There is about a two-year wait. The surgeon will tell you all about all the risks involved before you sign any consent form. However, in the meantime you *can* be treated with oestrogen, progesterone and a testosterone blocker as I've just said, but the effects of those could take many months to show. Nothing here will be a quick fix I'm afraid."

A flash of disappointment crossed Norma's features.

"I've waited so long for this, and I just want to get it over with *now*. I'm really motivated."

"I sympathise of course." Doctor Bryant nodded. "There is the private option, but procedures could add up to many thousands of pounds. This is an NHS clinic. You're lucky in a way that you can be treated in a clinic for adults. If you were a child or teenager there's only one UK clinic and you'd have to wait much longer."

Norma took another sip of water.

"I'll wait. I can't afford to go private. I haven't got a job."

"The wait will give you time to get used to living as a woman." Doctor Bryant tapped away at her keyboard. "Actually, I would say it's better this way."

Norma begged to contradict, but instead asked the first question that popped into her head.

"What happens just after surgery?"

"At first you will have a rod-like prosthesis in your vagina for five or so days to help the skin lining your new vagina to attach itself to the vaginal wall, and also a catheter in place for at least five days to allow the urethra to heal, as of course it needs to be in a different place." Doctor Bryant's eyes bored into Norma's as she swiveled her chair away from the computer. "You will have quite severe pain and internal bruises and will find it hard to sit, but of course you will be on strong painkillers and the discomfort will go in due course. We can provide rubber cushions to sit on. You will not be able to have a bath or immerse your body in water for at least eight weeks until the scars have healed. Most patients have to use dilators for some weeks afterwards, especially if there has not been enough penile tissue to create an adequately-sized vagina. Sometimes a further operation is needed to re-position the new labia. But don't worry about all this for now, because it's at least two years away."

"I see." Norma's shoulders slumped. "There's more to it than I thought."

"That's why you will need to be counselled." Doctor Bryant moved the wheels of her chair back towards the computer. "Vaginoplasty is irreversible and not a decision to take lightly."

Norma looked over at Doctor Bryant with interest.

"But at least I can start on the hormone treatment?"

"Yes, after counselling." Doctor Bryant nodded. "I have placed you on the waiting list. You will hear from Susan Meredith, our psychologist, within the next few weeks."

"Thank you." Norma relaxed a bit more. "Er…how will the hormone changes affect me?"

Doctor Bryant studied the display screen.

"Over a period of about six months there will be decreased libido and you will have decreased erections.

There will be a slowing of hair loss on your scalp, and you will have softer, less oily skin. You will have a redistribution of body fat, decreased muscle mass, and your breasts will start to develop."

"Great." Norma laughed. "I can't wait. Give it to me *now*."

"Sorry, no can do just yet." Doctor Bryant shook her head. "You will hear from Susan just as soon as an appointment is available. In the meantime you may wish to speak to your GP about freezing your sperm? Unfortunately we cannot do that for you. Again it would have to be done in the private sector at a cost."

"Oh no. I've no wish to become a parent. I'm too old now anyway. I'd look like the baby's grandfather...er...grandmother. Sorry, I'm still getting used to this myself."

The doctor stood up and extended her right hand across the desk."

"Of course, we'll leave that for now then. No more needs to be done at the moment. It was nice to meet you, Norma, and I'll get my secretary to type up the referral tomorrow."

"Thank you. "Norma rose to her feet and shook the doctor's hand, pleased that she had heard her new name. "I guess I'll see you again soon?"

"Absolutely." Doctor Bryant replied. "At least we've made a start now. After your counselling, don't forget to change your name by deed poll if you *are* set to become female. There are instructions online."

"Thanks." Norma replied. "I've already done it. Also, I want to lose weight so that I don't look like an all-in wrestler."

"Good." Doctor Bryant nodded. "I'm sure you'll feel better for it in the long run. It will no doubt help your diabetes too. And of course, not every one of my patients has the surgery. Some are happy just for the hormone treatment and the outward appearance of femininity."

"Oh no." Norma shook her head. "I want the surgery as well… the whole hog."

\*\*\*

She barely remembered the taxi ride. Her head whirled with mental images of dilators, catheters, urethras, labia, breasts and vaginas. On her arrival home Norma made no sound as she let herself into the house. Her mother dozed in the armchair as usual. The clock ticked on the wall the same as it always had, but Norma's humdrum life had changed beyond all recognition. She sank down onto the settee and closed her eyes; she had made the first tentative steps to becoming a *woman*, and it felt *good.*

# Chapter Sixteen - Norma

She dreaded her sister's visit, but Norma needed to get it over with. Gordon would be okay, but Ruth was another matter altogether. Norma applied more foundation to red, scraped skin on her cheeks in a vain attempt to hide any five-o'clock shadow, then smoothed strands of an ash blonde wig on its stand. She lifted the wig up with care, placed it into position on her head, and checked her transformation in the mirror into something she hoped might be half approaching female but not as outlandish as on her ginger days.

*What should she wear?* Norma had no intention to repeat the resemblance to a drag queen or to Freddie Mercury with his vacuum cleaner. She selected a pair of unisex jeans and trainers, and made a final choice of a frilly and floaty yellow top, hoop earrings, and sandals that sparkled in the lamplight. Okay, the top could have doubled for a sail in an emergency, but Norma was quite determined to be at least six dress sizes smaller by the time her penis was due for removal.

Voices out in the entrance hall alerted her to Ruth's arrival. Norma closed her eyes, said a short prayer out loud, and then with some determination strode out of the bedroom. Ruth, as usual, was the first to speak.

"You've *got* to be joking. You *are*, aren't you?"

Norma stood her ground, aware of the stares of three pairs of eyes.

"No, I'm perfectly serious."

"I don't half fancy you." Gordon burst out into uncontrollable laughter. "Sorry mate, but this is surreal!"

Norma's hands balled into fists. Ruth by this time had also dissolved into waves of hysteria; she clutched Gordon in an effort to stop herself falling on the floor. The pair of them giggled out of control, while Agnes held on to her trolley for dear life.

"What's so funny? What did you say, Gordon?"

"Look at him, Mum!" Ruth shouted as she wiped her eyes. "Have you ever seen anything so hilarious?"

"He can't help it." Agnes shrugged. "He wants to be a woman. God knows why. I'd much rather have been a man. Men have a much better deal out of life."

"Wanting to be a woman and actually *being* one are two different things." Ruth shook her head. "Give it up, Norman. You look utterly ridiculous."

Norma, red-faced with anger, strode closer to her sister.

"No, I *won't* give it up. Get used to it. Norma is here to stay. I don't care what you say or if you laugh yourself to death. I live now how I want to live, and you'll just have to get on with it."

She was proud of herself to be able to control enough anger to keep the floodgates at bay. Would a real woman have burst into tears by now? Norma knew her punch-your-lights-out anger might be more male-orientated, and a wave of despair washed over her at the long road ahead to femininity.

\*\*\*

"Are you sure you want to eat your dinner in your bedroom?"

Norma raised herself up on the bed and nodded.

"The pair of them are so rude. I'll come out when they've gone home."

"Take your tray off the trolley, dear, but it won't do you any good in the long run. You can't hide away in your bedroom all the time."

"I know, but if I'm in the same room as her I know I shall bop her one."

"That's not very ladylike." Agnes replied. "Anger management is the key here. Ladies don't go around bopping people."

"Mum… don't give me any more potatoes or chips." Norma set the dinner tray on her lap. "I want to lose weight."

"Yes, you're in a state." Agnes turned the trolley around and made towards the door. "If you were a bit slimmer you might look more feminine."

Norma sighed, looked down at the stodge on her plate, and made a face at her mother's retreating back. As usual

World War Three would erupt if she left any food, and Ruth and Gordon would dissolve into hysterics again if she came within sight of them on her way to flush any evidence down the toilet. No, it would have to be an out-of-the-window job and hope that the local wildlife liked potatoes.

\*\*\*

She had never had a proper friend, not even on the CB radio all those years ago. Norma had long since ceased to wonder why she had been born such a freak. A girlfriend to love and cherish would have been the ultimate goal, but hey, which self-respecting lesbian in her right mind would have wanted to start a relationship with a girl who had a penis? Male friends were out of the picture altogether; she chewed in a distracted way and recalled with horror the one and only job in the godawful warehouse which had lasted for just one morning. All she had wanted was for the Job Centre to have directed her towards the secretarial section, but with her looks, size and lack of qualifications, that would never have happened.

When her plate was empty she scrolled through several pretty faces on the *Gaydate* website, conscious of how her own face would look tucked in amongst all the others. Even after just a few hours of not shaving she would find it difficult to hide a five o'clock shadow. Norma sighed. It would be so much easier to stay hidden away in her bedroom, but she wanted that taste of life that everybody else seemed to manage to obtain without too much effort – somebody to love. Time was of the essence; she was now

57, and had diabetes. In the future there might even be a myriad of associated complications.

Truth be told, she could not wait another 2 years to become officially female. It was time to venture out and see what else her freaky life could offer. She was sick of the same old TV programmes in her bedroom.

Norma stared again at the screen, and then knocked herself on the forehead with the knuckles of her right hand. Yes she was gay, but she was also *transgender*. Perhaps a transgender website would be more up her street? Somewhat happier, she turned on the CD player and selected a hard rock compilation album. Music blasted out into the room, and the powerful beat sent a surge of determination through her body.

She divested herself of the unisex jeans and trainers, but kept the frilly top on. With an enigmatic smile about her lips she selected a short leather skirt, fishnet tights, and Doc Marten boots. She changed the blonde wig to her favourite ginger one. She sang along to 'Smoke on the Water' as she scrolled down a list of transgender dating sites. Somewhere out in Cyberworld there was a girl just right for *her,* and Norma needed to seek her out come hell or high water.

## Chapter Seventeen - Agnes

She would never know what had prompted her son to turn female at almost 58 years old, because to try and winkle any more information out of someone so incredibly secretive was nigh on impossible. However, it now made sense to her why Norman had played with girls at nursery school, and had preferred June and Ruth's dressing up box to his Action Man and toy cars. She also remembered how on more than one occasion she had found him wheeling Ruth's doll's pram around.

However, that was water under the bridge and now Norman was middle-aged and she was *old*, as old as old could be. Agnes stared down the corridor at Norman's closed bedroom door and then tried again to lever herself out of her armchair. She used the slow backwards and forwards rocking motion that had worked at other times but today had so far proved unsuccessful. To her horror she found herself still stuck in the chair after the seventh attempt.

"Help! Agnes began to panic. "Norman! Help! I can't stand up! I can't get out of the chair!"

Loud music emanated from the other side of the door. Agnes, desperate for a wee, pushed her trolley out of the way and then rocked again with an increased intensity. After the ninth attempt she pitched forwards with such force that she found herself face down on the carpet with her glasses dug into the bridge of her nose.

"Ouch! Help! Help!"

Her son's door stayed resolutely shut. Agnes inched towards the settee, but her knees refused to bend and years of deconditioning had made her arms too weak to be able to haul herself up. She floundered like a flapping fish on dry land. Agnes let go of her bladder in alarm.

"Somebody help me!"

The phone rested on a coffee table just out of reach. Agnes shuffled over to the table on her belly, pulled the phone down towards her and pressed Steven's speed dial button and the volume increase button. To her relief her son's mobile rang and his familiar voice comforted her as she laid on the floor not unlike a beached whale.

"Hi Mum, how are you?"

She wanted to cry, but pride got in the way.

"I'm on the floor and can't get up. Can you help me please?"

In an instant, Steven's apologetic tone told her all she wanted to know; no knight in polished armour would charge to her rescue in the near future.

"Oh…I can't get there, Mum. I'm in Manchester at the moment for a business meeting later on. Why don't you ask *His Ladyship*? What's he doing?"

"Norman's in his room with the door shut and the music turned up full. He can't hear me."

"I'll phone Ruth and Gordon, and if they're not around then I'll phone the paramedics for you, Mum. June won't be able to pick you up. Don't worry. If the bungalow's locked they'll probably knock on Norman's window as his room's in the front. I'll phone his mobile, but I don't hold out much hope there as he never answers it."

"Yes, that's why I phoned *you* instead." She started to weep despite her fierce resolution to keep any emotions in check. "Oh Steven, I've wet myself."

"Don't worry about that. Mum, I'll keep this line open and ring Ruth and Gordon for you from the office. Okay?"

"Okay." Agnes sniffed. "Thank you, son."

Certain that she was helpless, hapless, worthless, and a huge burden on her family, Agnes took her glasses off, wiped her eyes with the back of one hand, and kept the phone's receiver near her ear with the other. There was a spot of blood on the inside of the glasses. She took a few deep breaths and tried to compose herself.

"Steven?"

"Hi Mum, I'm still here." Steven replied straight away. "I think Ruth and Gordon might still be at work. The paramedics are on their way. They'll knock on Norman's window and he'll have to let them in. I'll phone later to see how you are."

"Thank you." Agnes wiped away tears of frustration. "Thanks very much."

There was nothing to do but wait. She could still hear music from the front bedroom. Agnes turned her face to one side, relaxed down into the carpet, and closed her eyes.

\*\*\*

"Mum!"

She had swum in the sea, but now somebody called her out of the water. Agnes, dripping wet, pushed her trolley along the shoreline.

"Mum!"

She woke with a start. Norman's legs in front of her were clad in fishnet tights, and there were what looked like diver's boots on his feet. Her underclothes were wet but she had not been in the sea, and as reality swam into focus it was patently obvious that neither had Norman.

"Oh…oh…"

A youngish man clad in a green uniform squatted down on his haunches. His voice sounded loud in her ears and rather over-jolly, as though he spoke to a child of tender years.

"Mrs Wicks, I'm Ian." His voice sounded loud in her ears and rather over-jolly, as though he spoke to a child of tender years. "I'm a paramedic. My colleague Donna and I will check that you are all right, and then we'll help you to get up."

"I didn't hear you calling, Mum." Norman squeezed the fingers of his left hand. "Sorry."

Agnes raised herself up on her two elbows.

"Of course you didn't. I'm absolutely fine. I fell and couldn't get up. My knees don't bend much anymore."

Agnes hoped nobody had noticed that she had wet herself. A motherly middle-aged woman checked her body and vital signs and then held her hand.

"Just call me Donna. Do you hurt anywhere?"

Agnes did not bother to reply. Her bones and joints had been ravaged by arthritis and osteoporosis over the previous twenty years, and so where should she start as regards her long list of aches and pains?

"I told you, I'm fine. Just help me up and give me my trolley, please."

Another strong pair of hands moved over her body. Donna spoke close to her ear.

"We'll put a ball underneath you that we'll inflate. It'll bring you upright, but slowly. Let me know if you have any pain in your hips when you stand up."

*Any more pain that she usually had?* Agnes wanted them all to go away so that she could change into clean underwear. Norman hovered around her like a wasp that needed to be swatted.

"What can I do, Mum?"

"You can answer your phone when somebody calls you and not play your music so loud."

There was no reply. From her vantage point on the ground she saw the diver's boots step away. A pump-like action caused something under her stomach to move her off the floor.

"Help!" Agnes threw both arms outwards. "I've got nothing to hold on to! I'm going to fall again!"

"No, you're fine. We've got you."

The diver's boots moved forward, and she felt Donna's arms steady her shoulders.

"Grab your mum under one arm, and I'll hold the other one."

Agnes was soon on her feet. A wet patch stained the carpet, but nobody mentioned it. She settled back in her armchair and took a deep breath.

"I need a different chair. It's a bit of a trouble to get out of this one."

"Your son…er…daughter will help you, now that he knows you have difficulty." Donna smiled and took a surreptitious glance at the Doc Marten boots and fishnet tights. " Would you like Social Services to come by and assess you for some proper mobility aids?"

"I think so." Agnes nodded. "I think the time has come."

"We'll get the ball rolling for you. Ian and I will sit with you a while longer, and then we'll go if you're okay."

"Thank you."

Agnes, ashamed of herself and mortified at the sight of her son in full drag before the two paramedics, silently raged against her frailties. She tried unsuccessfully to block Norman from sight, but still he stood there in front of her … as large as life.

"You can go back to your room, Norman. I don't need you now."

She gave him a glare to help him on his way. Relieved at the sight of the diver's boots as they promptly disappeared along the passageway, Agnes sat back in her chair, watched the paramedics pack up their kit, and willed them to go so that she could put on a pair of clean knickers in private.

## Chapter Eighteen - Norma

Norma, grateful the paramedics had not even twitched one facial muscle at the sight of her, dabbed at unsightly sweat beads on her forehead. However, the gender slip had not gone unnoticed. She closed the front door behind them and wished she could have been a fly on the wall as they got back into their car.

Her mother looked frail and tired, and there was a smell of hospital wards in the air. Norma wrinkled her nose; there was no way she, Norma, would ever sit in that armchair again.

"All right?"

She hoped the answer would be in the affirmative, as she had no idea what to do with an old lady in distress. Norma, relieved at her mother's nod, turned around and went back into her room.

\*\*\*

There was an unread email in her TransToDate inbox. Norma, intrigued, clicked on the message:

*'Hi Norma,*

*I saw your bio in the 'New Members' list. I'm Melanie. You can click on my profile to find out more about me, if you like. I live quite near you in Fulham. Fancy meeting up for a drink? Jack's Place, the pub near the tube station*

*has great music on Sunday nights. I can meet you outside?*
*Only £4 to get in.'*

Norma's stomach fluttered as she read the email. To actually have a like-minded friend, in fact *any* friend, would be something else. She clicked onto the link given, and read how Melanie was also male to female transsexual. The photo showed quite a pretty and feminine-looking person around forty years of age, with red hair, grey eyes, and not even a hint of a five o'clock shadow. Norma scratched her chin, which had the texture of sandpaper. She sighed as she typed a response.

*'Hi Melanie,*

*Thanks for getting in touch. I've only just 'come out' so to speak. I don't think I look very feminine at the moment, but I would love to meet you when I've lost a bit of weight. Give me a couple of months to get used to the new me, and I'll be in touch when I'm ready. I am so glad you've contacted me. I'm determined to turn my life around, whatever it takes. Will email soon. Best wishes, Norma.'*

Her thoughts on what to wear for such a momentous occasion were interrupted by a cry from the other side of the bedroom door. Norma could not bear to face the sight of her mother on the floor again. She picked up her phone and dialled Ruth's number, Steven's, and then June's to no effect. Another cry for help sounded from the front room, and great waves of panic washed over her. *What would she see when she opened the door? Would she have to clear up her mother's excreta or worse still, vomit? Would she have to make the paramedics come out yet again? What would they think of her if she had not even tried to get the old woman up from the floor?*

Just as her life had a chance to improve at last, her mother's infirmities might now start to hold her back. For the first time ever Norma had a sudden urge to pack up and leave home. *Why the hell had she left things this long? Why had she just coasted along and let her life chances slide into the abyss? More than half her natural lifespan was already over.*

She took a deep breath. *Where would she go? How could she survive just on benefits? How could she leave her needy mother on her own?* She knew she would not meet the criteria for a council house even if there wasn't a mile-long waiting list. She had no job, and no likelihood of ever getting one. *Who in their right mind would give a job to a freak of nearly sixty?* There was only one thing for it; she would have to make sure the house would not be sold on her mother's death and the money split up between her and her siblings. At least she would have somewhere to live. Her mother was frail. Who knows how much time she had left before the Grim Reaper wielded his scythe?

*She would have to persuade the old lady to change her will before it was too late otherwise she, Norma, would be out on her ear.*

Her mother's cries reached a crescendo. Norma sighed, got up from her chair, threw open the bedroom door and shouted down the passage.

94

"What's the matter?"

"I'm on the floor again!"

It was all down to *her* to have to deal with the sodden clothes and the wet chair and carpet, otherwise the house would reek of piss. Norma swallowed against a rising tide of bile and walked back into the front room. Her mother, helpless and angry, railed against her predicament.

"Help me up for God's sake! I want to get to the bathroom! Hurry up!"

It was obviously too late for that, as the damage had already been done. Norma put her hands underneath her mother's arms and lifted the frail body, light as a feather, to an upright position.

"Shall I help you to the bathroom?"

"No, of course not." Agnes shook her head. "I can see to myself. Just give me my trolley, will you?"

Norma, dismayed, chewed her lip then pushed the trolley in her mother's direction. As the old woman toddled off, Norma imagined the same scenario but instead with June or Ruth. Her sisters would without doubt have been invited into the bathroom to help, but Norma knew quite well why her mother had eschewed any aid.

*Would she ever be accepted into that most exclusive society... the one where everybody was most definitely female? Would she ever be recognised for the woman she really was?*

Norma sighed with the unfairness of it all. Her mother's words from long ago rang in her ears as Norma pulled up the sleeves of her blouse and filled a bucket with disinfectant… *'sometimes in life you have to do things that you don't want to do'.*

\*\*\*

Later that evening with her mother safe in bed, Norma searched for *Jack's Place* online. They had lived in Fulham for as long as she could remember, but to her surprise she had not known it was there. She was happy to see it was frequented mostly by the LGBT community. It was time to shed the pounds and then, scary as it seemed, force herself to get out into the world to see what it had to offer before it was too late.

## Chapter Nineteen - Hannah

Hannah Wicks yawned, put down her book, and gave a *tut* of annoyance at the sight of the display screen's number. She picked up the receiver and sighed. It was time to get her own back on her mother-in-law's assumption that Steven lived on his own. She gave a grin and spoke.

"Hello Norman."

There was a pause to enjoy the fact that the old girl had realised the tables had been turned.

"It's *Mum*."

Hannah heard the irritation in her mother-in-law's voice and welcomed a surge of joy.

"What can I do for you?"

"Can I speak to Steven, please?"

Agnes sounded frailer than she had done a couple of years before when Hannah had last spoken to her.

"He's in the shower, but I can take a message."

"I'd rather speak to *him*, so please ask him to ring me back."

The line went dead. Hannah replaced the receiver, and stuck two fingers up in the direction of the phone on her bedside table. She climbed out of bed and sauntered into the en-suite bathroom. Steven, naked and dripping, stepped out of the shower and grabbed a towel.

"Have you come to lust over my body?"

"Er…not quite." Hannah laughed. "Saint Agnes just rang. She won't tell *me* what she wants, only *you*. It's all a big secret, as usual, as again I'm still not worthy."

"Probably Norman's pissed her off again. Why don't you two kiss and make up?" Steven sighed. "Do it for *me*, if not for *her*, and maybe stop calling her *Saint* Agnes? That would be a good start."

"Only if *she* holds out the olive branch first." Hannah turned on her heel. "Let's face it…I'm not good enough for you, never have been, and never *will* be apparently. Whenever I used to ring her landline she always assumed it was you, and she's still doing it. It's as though I don't even live here."

"Don't start all that up again." Steven dried his hair with vigour, "You'll feel guilty when she's gone."

"Is that so?" Hannah looked back over her shoulder. "If your mother and I both went overboard, who would you save first?"

Steven shook his head.

"I'm not even going to answer that."

Hannah walked back into the bedroom. She already knew the answer anyway.

\*\*\*

She relaxed with her book in a nonchalant way, all the while with ears tuned for any facet of the conversation. Steve's non-committal grunts and one word answers so far had not done a thing to assuage her curiosity. When the call ended, Hannah marked her place and looked over at Steven.

"Well? What's the big secret?"

"Mum's finding it difficult to cope." Steven flopped back on the pillow beside her. "She can't get out of her armchair anymore without a huge struggle, and she's had a couple of falls. She doesn't know what to make of Norman now he's turned into a woman, and I think she's in a bit of a state."

"Oh." Hannah turned to look at him. "So what now, then?"

"She wants me to be there when Social Services come and assess her in a fortnight. They've sent her loads of forms to fill in and she's confused. She's asked the girls to be there too. I think the time has come where she realises she might have to go into a care home, or if not at least have some carers in during the day. She's worried about what will happen to Norman."

"Well, he's not coming *here.*" Hannah replied with haste. "I'm sure he's quite capable of looking after himself, if she would only let him. Will she have to sell the house?"

"Not if he still lives in it. Apparently he's been on at her to change her will and include him on the deeds. He wants their solicitor to come to the house and sort it out, but Mum's dragging her heels. If he owns half of the house, then it can't be sold without his permission. The rest of us will then miss out on our inheritance if he outlives us all."

Hannah nodded.

"It makes sense to stop the house being sold for care home fees though, because once the house *is* sold then *none* of you will get anything anyway. Norman's never had a job, so how can he buy a house?"

"Good question, he won't be able to." Steven replied. "As you say, he's not going to live with *us*. I don't want to meet any bloke on the landing in the mornings in high heels and fishnet tights."

Hannah snuggled up to Steven with a sigh of relief.

"Our spare rooms are for the grandchildren, even though we haven't got any yet."

"Billy's working on that." Steven chuckled. "Just as hard as he can. Er... you know what I'm going to ask though, don't you?"

"Just my luck to work for the council." Hannah turned off the bedside light. "I suppose you want *me* to help her fill in the forms?"

Steven gave her a kiss.

"I can't imagine that Ruth has the patience or June has the intelligence to trawl through all that paperwork, and I haven't got the time. Can you? For *me*? Pretty please?"

"Oh... bloody hell, okay, I'll give her a ring tomorrow and ask." Hannah closed her eyes. "If she says no, then she says no. I won't argue the toss. She'll have to get on with it."

\*\*\*

"Hello Steven."

Hannah stifled a scream, but decided to play the old lady at her own game.

"Hello Norman."

"It's *Mum*."

"And this is *Hannah*. Shall we start again?"

There was a brief pause at the other end. Hannah decided not to be the first one to break the silence.

"What do you want?"

Her mother-in-law's tone was icy. Hannah decided to reply in the same cold manner.

"Steve said you might need help with the council forms."

"Well, *Steven* is wrong."

"Okay." Hannah briefly considered repeating yet again her husband's preference for the shortened form of his Christian name. "I'll tell Steve you don't need any help then."

"Please do."

Hannah slammed the phone down, but her jubilation at being the first to end the call soon subsided. *What the hell had she ever done to be treated so contemptuously?* She kicked the table and mused on how she had married the favourite son for her sins, and the punishment for that was to be forever on the outskirts of Agnes' close-knit family. Her name was Wicks by marriage, but Hannah knew she would never be invited to the sacred inner enclave, no matter how hard she tried.

# Chapter Twenty - Norma

"Thanks for letting me have the cancellation slot, Doctor Meredith." Norma sat down and regarded the perfect example of femininity opposite her with envy. "I was certain I'd have to wait another few weeks."

"You're welcome. I'm pleased to meet you. Tell me a bit about yourself."

"Not much to tell really." Norma pulled a face. "I'm fifty seven and still live with my mother. That should tell you something. The family to be honest, have not been very supportive so far."

"Oh, I'm sorry to hear that. How long have you wanted to be a woman?"

"Always. I was born in the wrong body, you see. I'm male on the outside, but female inside my head."

"I understand." Susan Meredith opened a new patient case on her computer. "And how does that make you feel?"

"Like a freak." Norma shrugged. "It doesn't make for a happy life. I'm angry and sad at the same time. I want a girlfriend, but in a same-sex relationship. What girl would want *me* as I am now?"

"Have you been out and about as a woman?"

"Not yet." Norma admitted with a shake of her head. "I want to lose some weight first. I've come out to the family and they all laugh at me, but if I could be a bit slimmer I'd feel better about going to pubs and clubs. I feel as though everyone stares at me because I've let myself go over the years, and now I have to pay for it. I've started a diet, but so far have only lost a few pounds. Somebody contacted me on a dating website, but I don't feel confident enough to face her at the moment."

Susan Meredith nodded.

"It's usual for people to live in their preferred gender for up to two years before they have reassignment surgery. You'll then have plenty of time to get used to the new *you*. How do you feel about waiting that long?"

"I'll do what it takes." Norma stated with some conviction. "This is *it* for me, Doctor. I should have done this years ago. I've just *got* to be a woman!"

"To live true to oneself is what we all aim to do in the long run." Doctor Meredith took a sip of water. "It's the way to happiness and contentment for us all. After a few more counselling sessions I'll write a letter to your GP and you'll be able to begin your hormone therapy if you still want to."

"Oh yes." Norma nodded. "Doctor Bryant explained what would happen. I don't need any more counselling. I *know* I want to be a woman."

"What do you know about the effects of hormone treatment?"

Norma hid waves of impatience she knew would get her absolutely nowhere.

"Breasts will grow in a few months. Muscle strength will decrease, and so will libido. I'll have softer skin, but it won't change my physical shape. I've already lost my hair, so no amount of oestrogen will bring it back. But hey… some kind soul invented wigs."

Doctor Meredith smiled.

"And you accept all these?"

"Of course." Norma agreed at once. "It's what I want."

"You might be more prone to blood clots, gallstones, acne, and even more weight gain as well."

"Bring it on." Norma shrugged. "But not the weight gain."

"I'd like to see you a couple of times more, just to confirm." Susan Meredith scribbled a few notes on a piece of paper. "I can see you're eager, but we need to make sure. I'd like to know that you've been out to meet that person on the dating site by the time you come back in a month's time"

"Oh God." Norma chuckled. "Okay. I'll do my best, but I want to lose some weight first."

"No excuses, just do it."

\*\*\*

Her palms were sweaty, and her mouth was unpleasantly dry. Norma adjusted her wig one more time, and hoped the pashmina would hide the results of too many stodgy dinners. She had definitely been more energetic since she had eschewed potatoes and bread, but hated the ever-present hunger and her failure to lose only four pounds since her meeting with Doctor Meredith.

A tall, slim woman with shoulder-length red hair stood under an umbrella outside *Jack's Place* as Norma rounded the corner into the High Street. She noted the woman's suede ankle boots, above-the-knee skirt, and bomber jacket. As she approached the pub she made a conscious effort to get her breathing under control.

"Hi, are you Melanie?"

"Yeah, and I'm freezing my arse off here."

Norma, surprised at the pleasant feminine voice, laughed in relief.

"I'm Norma, and I'm too nervous to feel cold."

"Come on in, then." Melanie folded up her umbrella. "There's no good time of the year to loiter about in Fulham High Street. I've already had two offers from kerb crawlers while I've been standing here."

The noise and heat from numerous bodies hit her as soon as they walked through the door. Norma swallowed with fright and kept her eyes on Melanie's back as she followed her up to the bar.

"What do you want to drink?" Melanie shouted over her shoulder."

Norma, mind blank with terror, blurted out the first thing that came into her head.

"Lemonade please."

"Blimey, you're cheap to take out."

Norma made use of the nearest bar stool and sat down gratefully to rest jelly-like legs.

"Sorry, I'm a bit nervous. I haven't been out much."

"I'm just yanking your chain." Melanie gave Norma's shoulder a pat and then looked towards a slightly overweight man in a bright orange suit. "Jack, this is Norma. Norma, meet Jack Metcalf. He charges exorbitant prices, but he's lovely."

"Hi, Jack. "Norma held out her right arm. "Pleased to meet you."

She felt her hand squeezed in a firm grip.

"Enchanted. Haven't seen you in here before."

She relaxed somewhat. Nobody around had even bothered to look her way.

"I'm a bit of a late developer. Love the suit, by the way."

Jack laughed.

"But you got there in the end, eh? First drink is free, despite what Melanie says, and oh… I often have an orange day."

"Thanks for the free drink." Norma, surprised, looked at Jack and raised one thumb. "Just a lemonade for now please."

Melanie took the drinks from Jack and indicated with a nod of her head towards an empty table at the back of the pub.

"Come on, I can see somewhere to sit. There's a big crowd in here tonight."

A band began to tune up. Norma, apologetic, squeezed past a table full of giggling women, but only one showed even the slightest interest. She sank down into a chair, pleased to be in a quiet corner.

"So…" Melanie took a gulp of beer. "Tell me about yourself."

"Nothing to tell, really." Norma grimaced. "I just want to live as a woman now. I've denied it for so many years for an easy life."

"Yeah, we all get to that stage." Melanie crossed her legs. "I used to be a fireman, and macho as hell, because that's how the other guys were. One day I couldn't live a lie anymore. I gave in my notice and saw a shrink, and … *now* look at me."

Norma sipped her lemonade and tried not to stare too hard at her new friend.

"All I want to do is lose all this flab and look a bit more feminine."

"And you'll do it, because you're motivated at last and you *want* to do it badly enough." Melanie nodded. "The guys at work took the piss out of me something rotten when I came out, but after I left the fire service I got an office based job with more girls around and I've never been happier. Girls are more understanding, I think."

Norma sighed.

"I had a job once, well… just for a morning in a warehouse. I couldn't relate to the blokes there at all. They got hold of me and pulled my jeans and underpants down in some bizarre initiation ceremony. I ran out the door and never went back. I wanted to die. I would love to work in an office, but now I've not got the confidence to apply for vacancies."

She shuddered at a sudden recollection of the four Neanderthals. However, she was now totally at ease in Melanie's company. She sat back in her chair and looked around at the clientele.

"Is everybody here LGBT?"

"Not everybody... some are *cis*." Melanie shook her head. "But most of them are. I don't know about you, but I prefer to be with them. They're more open minded and forgiving."

"You're right." Norma agreed. "I just feel like a fucking freak. What's *cis*, by the way?"

Melanie leaned in towards Norma.

"Don't *ever* feel that way. You are what you are, and nobody has the right to call you a freak!"

Norma blinked away a tear and took a shaky breath.

"Thank you. Thank you very much."

Melanie patted her arm.

"*Cis* are people whose gender corresponds with their birth sex."

"That's another thing I've learned." Norma sniffed. "I wish mine did."

\*\*\*

"So... we last met about a month ago, is that right?"

Doctor Meredith took a brief glance at her notes and then looked up.

"Yes." Norma nodded. "And I've lost half a stone since then."

Susan Meredith smiled.

"Good for you. How have you got on otherwise?"

"Better. I've been a couple of times to an LGBT pub on the High Street with a new friend, Melanie. She accepts me as I am. They *all* do in there. It's great."

"Well done, Norma. It's hard to build a social life at first, but it seems you're well on the way. How about your family? How have they taken to you now that you're *out*?"

"Not good." Norma sighed. "I'm still Norman, and *will* be forever I expect."

"Give them time."

"What if they *never* accept the new me?" Norma tapped her foot on the floor with some impatience. "Everything's a battle with them. Maybe if I start the hormone treatment soon it will tell them I'm serious?"

"Yes it will, but once you start and your breasts begin to grow, then you won't be able to go back."

"I don't *want* to go back." She gave a snort of disapproval. "It's time to go *forwards*. Norman is *gone* as far as I'm concerned. I've already changed my name by deed poll."

Susan Meredith nodded in agreement.

"I must advise you that the hormone treatment could make you infertile. Your GP can help you with advice about gamete storage - the ability to harvest and keep your sperm for future use. This isn't available on the NHS."

"I'm too old to be a parent now." Norma shook her head. "And I don't really like children much, to tell you the truth. I still have to find out about *me*, let alone having to look after a baby at the same time. The sooner I can have hormone treatment, the better I shall like it."

"You seem quite determined, I can tell." Doctor Meredith took a consent form out of her file. "Okay, with your agreement then perhaps it *is* time to move on."

"I give my consent a thousand times over." Norma laughed. "Yes, yes, yes, I'll sign!"

## Chapter Twenty One - Steven

"What have you got under there? Chicken fillets?"

Steven's mouth twitched as he tried to hold back the laughter. His brother's small titties were somewhat mesmerising, not to mention the blonde wig, ankle boots, calf-length skirt and jumper which sported a low V neck and a chest full of stubble.

"No. They're real. I've been on hormone therapy for three months now."

"You look ridiculous."

"Thanks. I don't need to listen to this. I'm going to my room now to wait for a call."

Steven stared as Norman, shoulders back and head held high, made his way out into the passage. He looked across at his mother who sat straight-backed in her new all-singing-all-dancing chair.

"Is he all there? Whatever's happened to him?"

"What?"

The old girl looked tired out. Steven squatted down beside his mother and put his mouth to her ear.

"Is Norman the full shilling?"

"Don't forget, Steven, we mustn't call him Norman because he'll get upset. We have to call him Norma now."

"But he's a *bloke*." Steven shook his head. "He's a bloke who wears women's clothes."

Agnes shrugged.

"*I* know that and *you* know that. But he's convinced he's a woman."

"How does he treat you?" Steven put an arm around his mother's shoulders. "Does he help out more?"

Agnes yawned.

"Not that I've noticed, but the council has sorted out some help for me. Norman didn't like Rita at first, but now he's quite taken with her. In fact I think he's got a crush on her. She cleans around a couple of times a week, takes out the rubbish and changes the beds. She's a godsend."

"Yeah, June mentioned that when I spoke to her last week. Are you still happy to live here with him?"

Agnes nodded.

"Now I've got some help, it's better. I want to keep my independence for as long as possible. All I need to do now is cook meals, see to myself, and take the washing out of the machine and put it in the tumble drier."

Steven wanted to wrap his arms around the frail body, but had been raised in the undemonstrative way peculiar to all his siblings.

"What about that solicitor?"

"Oh yes, I forgot." Agnes touched her forehead with the palm of one hand. "Norman's been on at me about that, but I want to do the right thing for *all* of you, not just *him*. Give the man a ring and all of you come round one evening. I'll leave you to sort it out. I can't seem to get my head around things as quickly as I used to anymore."

His strong, capable mother was crumbling away bit by bit. Steven exhaled a shaky breath.

"Okay." He nodded. "It'll be easy to do. For a price the solicitor can change the deeds to tenants-in-common. You'll own one half of the house and we'll own the other half. In that way the house cannot be sold unless we all give permission."

"Good." Agnes reached out and touched her son's fingers. "Go and tell Norman."

He could not remember the last time he had held his mother's hand. Steven instinctively reached forward and planted a soft kiss on the old lady's forehead, who looked at him in great surprise.

"Will do." He stood up. "I'll do it now."

\*\*\*

He could hear his brother on the phone to person or persons unknown. Steven tried the doorknob, which failed to move.

"Open the door, Norman. I want to speak to you."

"In a minute."

He stared at the closed door and willed the phone call to end. When at length his brother ceased to speak, Steven kicked the door with one foot.

"Open up *now*, Norman! It's about this house."

In a flash he heard the key turn in the lock. He stood face to face with a brother he now did not seem to know at all.

"What about it? And the name's *Norma*. I don't know how many times I've got to tell you."

"Well... *Norma*." Steven gazed at the ghastly vision before him and tried not to grimace. "I'll organise for the solicitor to come and see Mum, so as to turn over half of the house to the rest of us legally as tenants-in-common. We'll be here together when he's free to visit."

"You'll all kick me out, I can see that coming." Norma sighed. "You can't wait to get rid of me, can you?"

Steven almost nodded. The answer his brother did not want to hear was on the tip of his tongue.

"None of us will be able to sell the house without the others' permissions, you'll be pleased to hear."

"Terrific."

The door slammed shut. Steven gave it a mighty kick and then turned away.

## Chapter Twenty Two - Rita

36 Crozier Road was always the first bungalow she went to on Mondays and Thursdays, just to get it over with. Rita Costello reluctantly rang the doorbell and wished she had been born with shedloads of money instead of good looks. To her dismay Norman threw the door open almost at once.

"*Do* come in. We've been looking forward to your visit all weekend!"

Rita inwardly cringed, then rushed past the freak into the hallway.

"Where do you want me to start?"

"Let's go into the kitchen first and have a cup of tea."

She looked at her watch.

"Sorry, but I have other houses to clean this morning so I can't hang about. Besides, Mrs Wicks won't want me to sit down and drink tea. That's not what she pays me for."

"She won't mind. I insist."

Rita's heart sank. The last thing she wanted was to be followed about by Norman bloody Wicks in his dress and high heels as he attempted to chat her up. Her half-Latin temperament had a sudden flare.

"Look, Norman, I've just had a cup of tea before I left home and I don't want another one. I'll go and ask your mum where she wants me to begin."

"It's *Norma*. My name is *Norma*. Don't forget that."

"I won't."

Rita almost ran into the front room, where the old lady dozed in her chair.

"Hello Mrs Wicks!" Rita shouted. "How are you today?"

She saw Agnes Wicks' eyes open with a start.

"Oh... oh, hello Rita." Agnes appeared momentarily dazed. "I forgot you were coming today."

"Do you want me to get the vacuum cleaner out?"

"No, not today. The beds need clean sheets, there's a bit of washing up from breakfast, and you can dust around if you like."

"Okay." Rita tried not to let her smile turn into a grimace. "I'll start with the beds then."

Aware that Norman had heard their conversation and had disappeared back into his bedroom, Rita decided to tackle the most unpleasant task first. She turned on her heel, walked along the passage, and rapped on the bedroom door that she hoped would stay locked.

"Hey Rita, what can I do for you?"

She noticed the change of clothes; fishnet tights, short leather skirt and low cut top. She ignored an urge to run.

"Agnes wants me to change your bedclothes."

"Sure, sure. Come in."

The room smelt fusty and there was an overpowering stench of perfume mixed in. Three plastic heads on the dressing table each sported a wig and regarded her with sightless eyes.  Rita swallowed the urge to retch.  She walked to the side of the bed furthest away and pulled off the duvet cover, sheet and pillowcases in record time.

"I'll just put these in the washing machine."

"Oh, can you put some clean ones on first?"

He stood by the door to block her escape.  She bundled all the linen under one arm and considered whether a swift kick in the balls might cause him to either move or to punch her in the face.

"Show me where you keep the clean bedclothes."

"Don't you remember?"  Norman looked at Rita in amusement.  "After all, they're in the same place as they were before."

He had not moved his sizeable bulk from the door.  Rita deposited the dirty laundry on the floor and made her way to his built in wardrobe.

"Silly me.  Perhaps I've got Alzheimer's."

"No, not a pretty young thing like you."

Rita yearned to escape into the fresh air.  She opened the wardrobe door to see a full rail of women's clothes.  She pulled out a drawer and whipped out a new set of bed linen.

"I'll have these on in no time."

"I'll help you."

As if on skates she moved around to the side of the bed nearest to the door and picked up a clean sheet.  She kept her eyes cast downwards as a hand grabbed the opposite corner.

"Would you like to come with me to Jack's Place down in the High Street? It's a great night out with live music."

"Thanks, but no thanks." Rita shook her head. "My husband wouldn't like it."

"I didn't know you were married. You don't wear a wedding ring."

She heard the disappointment in his voice and reckoned she could make it to the door in less than two seconds flat.

"Yeah, I'm married. Got two kids at school as well. I don't wear my wedding ring while I'm at work in case it gets damaged."

With his now flattened mood, the offer of help vanished in a trice. Through her peripheral vision Rita saw him move to a chair by the window and stare out in a rather doleful fashion. She shook a new duvet cover into place and plumped up two pillows in their clean cases. She grabbed the pile of dirty laundry once more, and then opened the bedroom door and rushed out with the hint of a grin on her face. Hopefully the freak would not bother her again.

## Chapter Twenty Three - Norma

Norma looked at herself in the mirror with some degree of satisfaction. The diet, agonising as it was, had started to pay off. Living true to herself had given her the confidence she had lacked for so long. She had lost some weight, and her breasts had continued to grow in size. After two months on hormone therapy she no longer needed bra fillers, her skin was softer, and there had recently been a welcome reprieve in her chronic sexual frustration. She could now squeeze into the skirt that had been too small and which she had nearly sent back. Three new wigs sat resplendent on stands. She picked her favourite one and carefully arranged wispy strands of ginger hair around her face.

Happier than she had been for a long time, she performed a little pirouette and watched the folds of her skirt flare out in the mirror's reflection. She felt like a whole *woman*! She gave a contented sigh and twirled towards the bedroom door. All she needed now was to get rid of the hated dick.

She smiled at her mother as she sat in her usual armchair.

"Can you see an improvement yet?"

The old lady regarded her with a gimlet eye.

"In what?"

Norma lifted her arms up and did a quick spin on one heel.

"In *me*. In my figure?"

Agnes shook her head.

"Not that I've noticed. You look like the back end of a bus."

Waves of anger crashed over her.

"I'm trying to sort my life out and you give me no encouragement whatsoever!"

"Look. I want to tell it to you straight." Agnes shrugged. "You'll *never* look like a woman. You're a bloke in drag and that's the reality of it. And there's another thing... Rita's quit, but she didn't say why. Now we've got to wait until the council sends us another cleaner."

She needed to get out of the house. Norma hurried along the passage back to her bedroom. She grabbed her coat and bag and without another word ran outside.

\*\*\*

The High Street bustled with life, and Jack's Place was open for lunch. In the past she would never have been able to pluck up enough courage to go inside on her own, but today she would make the effort. Melanie was at work, and Norma needed to be amongst her own people. She took a deep breath and pushed the door open. Nobody showed the slightest bit of interest, and that was fine as far as she was concerned. Jack, resplendent in a banana yellow waistcoat and trousers, beamed from behind the bar.

"Hi Norma. Nice to see you. What'll it be?"

She smiled, pleased that Jack had remembered her name, and even better, treated her like a normal person.

"Could I see your lunch menu please, Jack?"

"Sure."

She knew her mother would have lunch on the table at the dot of one o'clock, but she decided to deal with the fallout later on. That precise moment she needed to feel part of a community, and right now she belonged on a bar stool at Jack's Place. Norma perused the menu.

"Chicken salad please and a tonic water."

Jack took the menu and nodded.

"Coming up. Have you lost weight?"

"Yeah, nearly a stone. Only another forty four to go."

She liked the way Jack laughed at her comment.

"I live to eat, darlin', it's the right way to be. I don't like to exist on just lettuce leaves and air. Eat what you want to and be happy. In that way you don't think about food all the time."

"Hah, right now I need to eat lettuce leaves."

She relaxed, sipped her drink, and enjoyed the pleasant atmosphere. She acknowledged a smartly dressed middle aged man with a shock of greying hair as he approached the bar. The man stood beside her and held up one hand to gain Jack's attention.

"Can I buy you a drink?"

Norma, surprised, was momentarily stumped for words. She nodded.

"Oh …just tonic water, thanks."

"Haven't seen you in here before."

"Umm… no. I've only been in a couple of times with my friend Melanie."

"I'm Leslie."

"Norma. Pleased to meet you."

Leslie held out his arm.

"Likewise, I'm sure."

Norma shook the proffered hand, hoped her wig was on straight, and wondered why a good looking man like Leslie would want to chat her up. *Did he fancy her? Was she attractive to men?*

"Do you come in here a lot?"

She wanted to cringe after such a banal question, but was stumped for something more meaningful to say.

"Most days, yeah. I work nearby and usually have my lunch here."

Norma nodded.

"I've just ordered a salad."

"Oh well, I'll order my food and sit with *you* if I may?"

Another tonic water appeared in front of her. Leslie perched on the next bar stool and sipped a pint of lager.

"Fancy coming to the pictures tonight? There's always something good on at the Odeon."

Norma almost fell off her stool in shock. It had taken upwards of fifty eight years, but finally somebody had asked her out.

"Sure. What's on?"

"Don't know yet, but I'll find out. Wait for me outside Jack's Place and I'll pick you up about seven."

She met Leslie's eyes with confidence; two new friends in such a short time was unprecedented. Her pulse raced as she made small talk, and her cheeks flushed with keen anticipation of the evening ahead.

\*\*\*

She waved as Melanie tottered towards her along the High Street in impossibly high heels.

"Hey Norma. Are you waiting for me?"

Norma raised an arm to greet her friend.

"Er, not quite. I met a guy here, Leslie, at lunch time today. He said he'd pick me up at seven and then we'd go to the pictures."

To her surprise, Melanie grimaced.

"Leslie Stephenson? Good looking? Middle aged?"

"Don't know." Norma shrugged. "He didn't tell me his surname. Yeah, quite handsome though."

Melanie shook her head.

"There's no way you'll go to the cinema. Haven't seen him for a while, but he's obviously been in cruising for new meat. He does that sometimes. He'll probably suggest a ten mile detour to Hampstead Heath."

"What for?"

"Blimey, you don't get out much, do you?" Melanie gave a snort of laughter. "He's gay, sweet pea, and he's taken a shine to *you*."

"Oh, God." Norma, confused, followed Leslie's car with her eyes as it came to a halt outside the bar. "But I'm a *woman*."

"Well...almost." Melanie replied. "I expect he's only interested in the one bit that isn't."

"But... how did he know?"

Melanie remained tactfully silent. Norma did not know whether to laugh, cry, or kick Leslie in the bollocks.

## Chapter Twenty Four - Steven

"I'll get it."

Steven checked the display screen then picked up the landline receiver.

"Hi Mum. What's up?"

"It's Norman."

Steven sighed.

"What's up with him *now*?"

"Something's happened and he's depressed. He won't eat, and he won't come out of his room. I know he's trying to lose weight but I don't think he ate *anything* yesterday, unless he's got a secret stash of chocolate somewhere."

"What can *I* do?" Steven replied. "He won't listen to *me*."

His mother's shaky voice filtered down the line.

"Take him to the pub. Butch him up a bit. Try and get him out of this ridiculous notion that he's a woman. Get him to talk to other blokes. I'm sure he'll be happier then."

Steven flinched as Hannah passed by and tweaked one of his nipples.

"Will you stop that?"

"What?"

"No, not you, Mum" Steven laughed. "Oh, you've definitely given me a bit of a job there. We're hardly bosom buddies... no, perhaps I shouldn't mention bosoms."

"Just do your best. Come for dinner tomorrow and take him out afterwards."

"What about Hannah?"

He was aware of a momentary pause.

"Okay... if she wants to come."

"I'll ask her." Steven put his hand over the receiver. "Babe, do you want to go to dinner at Mum's tomorrow night?"

He lip read *'up yours'*, then grinned as his wife stuck two fingers up in his direction.

"She's busy tomorrow."

"What a shame."

His mother's relief was evident. Steven wondered whether his wife or his mother would crack first and hold out the olive branch.

\*\*\*

Steven was at a loss as to what to say. His brother pushed some peas around his plate in a desultory fashion with a fork held in one meticulously manicured hand.

"You've lost some weight."

He was pleased to see Norman lift his head and manage a weak smile.

"Thanks. I've tried really hard."

"Want to go down the pub after dinner, mate?"

"As long as we can go to Jack's Place on the High Street."

"That's a gay pub, right?" Steven shook his head. "Don't think I'd fit in."

"Yeah, you'd be frightened to drop the soap in the Gents', wouldn't you?"

Steven picked up on the unfriendly riposte and chuckled, unconcerned. He looked across at his mother who, head down, seemed oblivious to the conversation while she ate. He decided to lay his cards on the table once and for all.

"Something bothering you?"

He watched his brother put down his fork, stand up and smooth down his skirt.

"Plenty. For a start, why don't you call me *Norma*?"

"Because for fifty odd years I've called you *Norman*." Steven shrugged. "You don't *look* like a Norma, because, let's face it, you're a *Norman*. Oh, sod it, come on then, *Norma*, let's wash the dishes for Mum and then you can take me to the pub."

He raised one thumb to his mother and got to his feet.

"Thanks for the dinner, Mum. We'll clear the crockery away and then we'll go out for a drink."

"Okay. Make sure Norman's not back late."

"I don't do washing up." Norma made for the door. "I've just painted my nails."

With some difficulty Steven subdued a mental image of himself as he held his brother's head down in hot, soapy washing up water.

"You do tonight if you want to go out with *me*."

Norma shook her head.

"I *don't*. It was *your* idea."

Steven sighed.

"Just pick up a tea towel and dry. I'll wash. After all, you don't want your nail varnish to start peeling, do you?"

"Don't take the piss."

They stood side by side at the sink. Steven remembered a four year old who rode a red tricycle, played with tin soldiers and raced toy cars around a track, although a couple of times he recalled how Norman had pushed their sisters' dolls' prams about. As far as he knew at the time, as far as they *all* knew, Norman had enjoyed being a boy. He passed a plate to fingers draped in rings and trimmed with long purple nails, and wondered what the hell had happened to his brother.

## Chapter Twenty Five - Steven

Steven made a beeline for an empty table well away from two men who kissed with abandon in one corner. He gulped a swig of beer and sat down with his back towards the rest of the clientele.

"D'you want a beer then, mate?"

His brother took a seat opposite.

"I prefer non-alcoholic cocktails. Jack's very good at cocktails."

"Yeah, I bet he is."

Norma sipped a brightly coloured drink.

"What's that supposed to mean?"

"Probably means he's good at fixing drinks?"

Steven chewed on a fingernail, uncomfortable in such alien surroundings. Three obvious drag queens on a table to his left laughed; a hearty roar assaulted his eardrums. A juke box played '*Stand by Your Man*'. His brother waved to a Julian Clary lookalike who had burst in through the door

"That's Larry."

"Is that so?" Steven downed half a pint in one go. "He looks more like a Lisa. Look, Norman, when the hell will you come to your senses? Mum's worried about you. We're *all* worried about you, come to that." He waved one arm around the room. "Do you really want this kind of life?

I mean… you don't even know which bog to use now, do you?"

Norma fixed Steven with a piercing stare.

"If it's any of your business, I use the disabled toilets."

Steven sat back and ran one hand through his hair in a distracted way.

"Christ.. but you're a *bloke*! What have you done to yourself?"

"Do you feel like a bloke in your head?" Norma pointed one finger at her forehead. "*Do* you?"

"Of course." Steven shrugged. "Why wouldn't I?"

Norma's right hand balled into a fist and hit the table with a solid thump.

"Well, *my* brain tells me I'm female. It's *always* told me I'm female. I played with cars and tin soldiers, but I wanted *dolls*. There's nothing I can do about it, except to *be* female. It's what I'm trying to do, but lots of ignorant bastards don't seem to understand."

Steven ignored the jibe; he had a great urge to jump up and bolt out the door. He glanced away from his brother's earnest expression, and to his dismay saw the Julian Clary lookalike on a direct path towards their table.

"Hi Larry." Norma pulled out a chair. "Nice to see you again."

Larry gazed with approval in Steven's direction.

"And who's this little treasure, may I ask?"

"He's my big brother." Norma laughed. "Keep your mitts off."

Steven gave Larry a withering look.

"If one of your mitts comes anywhere near me, I'll bite the fucking thing off. This is a private party."

"Tsk, tsk, such violence." Larry shook his head. "See you soon, Norma. I know when I'm not wanted."

Norma sighed in Larry's direction as he retreated towards the bar.

"What did you have to go and say that for? He's harmless."

"Stop this before it's too late." Steven hissed. "Everyone will laugh at you. You'll end up a freak."

Norma's eyes stung with angry tears.

"I already am, brother. You'll never know what it's like to be female in a man's body, so count your blessings. You don't look down and see a dick where a dick shouldn't be."

Steven recoiled at the grotesque sight of his brother's mascara, which ran in rivulets down his cheeks. He wracked his brain for something to say.

"Want another drink?"

"No. I want to go home."

"That's absolutely fine with me." Steven stood up. "I started the evening off with the intention to try and get you to change your mind, but I can see I'm wasting my time."

Norma wiped her eyes.

"Help me, for God's sake. It would be great for somebody in the family to actually be on my side."

They filed through the crowd. Norma gave a desultory wave to Jack and then opened the main door. Steven enjoyed a rush of cool evening air.

"I'll walk back with you and say goodbye to Mum."

"I bet *she* put you up to this, didn't she?"

Steven stared into shop windows as, side by side, they traipsed along Fulham High Street.

"Of course not. She's too old to get her head around it, but perhaps this evening has made me understand it all a bit better."

"I hope so." Norma sniffed. "I didn't ask to be born this way, you know. It's why I've never worked, but everybody thinks I'm lazy."

"Yeah?" Steven looked at Norma in surprise. "Really?"

Norma gave a brief nod.

"Yeah. Mum and Dad expected me to get a trade, like you. I don't have an engineering mind, and I'm not creative in any way. The only thing I've ever been good at is word processing and spelling. How could I tell them I wanted to be a secretary? How will *that* pay for a mortgage? To add to that, which boss who needs a PA is going to pick *me* over a pretty young girl? Over the years it's just been easier to live off the state, but with benefits it's hard to live an independent life. Do you see where I'm coming from now?"

"Sure."

Steven knew his mother would be eager to learn the evening's outcome. To his utter surprise he looked at the hulking lump of a woman that was his trans-sister, and let a wave of empathy wash over him.

"Give me time, Norma. I'll get used to it."

He was rewarded with the hint of a smile.

"Thank you."

\*\*\*

"How did you get on?"

Steven grimaced and looked towards Norma's closed bedroom door.

"He … she… wants to be a woman. He won't change his mind. It's all very confusing I know, but I think we ought to call him Norma."

Agnes gave a snort of disapproval.

"I brought him up as a boy because he *was* a boy. Now he's a *man*. Whoever has heard of a man called *Norma*?"

"His body is male, sure." Steven nodded. "But in his head he's female. Something went wrong inside the womb by the sound of it."

"So it's *my* fault?" Agnes regarded Steven with an icy stare. "Does he blame *me*?"

"No, of course not, Mum. We all know that you don't have any control over a developing baby."

"Perhaps it's something I ate, or didn't eat." Agnes shrugged. "They wanted to give me iron tablets, but iron bungs me up."

"Forget it. He… *she* is working it out. Forget it."

# Chapter Twenty Six – Norma

"You look very well. How have you got on since we last met?"

Norma smiled at Susan Meredith.

"I've been a bit down recently. Things aren't happening as quickly as I would like."

Susan nodded in sympathy.

"I did try and warn you, but don't lose your resolve. However, on a positive note I can see you've definitely shed some weight."

"Thanks. It's so hard to get people to take me seriously though."

"Of course it will be hard, when they've only ever seen you as a man. Give it time and stay focused. How do you feel on the hormone treatment?"

"I've definitely lost some libido, which is good in my single state." Norma chuckled. "I've also had some acne, which is a bit of a drawback. On a positive note I do have some breast development, and I've met a casual friend, Melanie, via a Trans dating website."

"Good for you. With your permission I'll examine you. After that the nurse can take some blood tests today to check your liver enzymes, the amount of red cells you have, and also your oestrogen level and the amount of fat there is in your blood. I'm sure all will be well, but we will have to check these things pretty regularly now."

"Of course."

"We'll let you know of any abnormal results, but if you don't hear from us you can take it that everything's okay and that we'll see you again in a couple of months' time. After the examination, just go back out into the waiting room and I'll tell our nurse to give you a shout. Oh, and I'll write to your GP to invite you for breast screening. Any other questions?"

"Just one." Norma replied. "Is there any way I can make my voice sound more like a woman's?"

"There are ways." Susan Meredith nodded. "Again, just speak to the nurse and she can give you some leaflets and a couple of exercises to do, or we can refer you to Speech and Language therapy back at the hospital."

\*\*\*

Norma, now a stone and a half lighter, spooned the remnants of a rather delicious sorbet and took care not to smudge her Pink Petal lipstick. She now spent most lunchtimes at Jack's Place. Sometimes Melanie or Larry appeared for a chat, but on other occasions she sat at the bar, swapped banter with Jack, and enjoyed a stress-free healthy lunch amongst people of her own ilk.

"That was a lovely meal, Jack." Norma handed over her bank card. "You've got busier at lunchtimes now."

"Yeah, I could do with more help. It always gets crazy when we head towards summer. Don't suppose you fancy doing a couple of hours from mid-day to two o'clock on Fridays and weekends by any chance?

Norma replaced the card in her purse and looked up at Jack in surprise.

"Me?"

"Yeah, *you*." Jack laughed. "You sit there on your backside every lunchtime. You can earn some money instead if you like, but I can assure you that your arse won't ever touch that seat."

"I've never worked in a bar." Norma replied. "I've never worked anywhere, come to that."

"You look like a strong girl. I'm sure you can pull a pint the same as anyone, and collect empties from the tables. You'll also take some lunch orders when customers come up to the bar. I have a few girls to wait tables, and a cellar man to change the barrels over downstairs, so you won't have to do that. Nine pounds an hour, and you can start on Friday at twelve o'clock. I think that's fair. I usually take on a couple of summer workers as well. Belinda Smithson will come back soon, and she worked here last year. You'll have some company in a week or two. You'll lose loads more weight as well, because you'll rush around like a blue arse fly."

"I'll have to check how it works with my benefits, but I think I can work up to sixteen hours a week."

"Yes you can." Jack nodded. "What d'you say then? You can have your lunch here after your shift ends if you like, and you can have it at a discount."

Norma laughed, and at that precise moment felt strong enough to take on the world.

"Okay, I'll give it my best shot. What do you want me to wear?"

"The same uniform as all the other staff. There's a red polo shirt with a logo, and either a black skirt or trousers. I'll supply two shirts, two skirts, and two pairs of trousers if you give me your size. As you'll be on your feet a lot you can wear trainers or flat shoes."

"Thanks Jack for this chance. I'm a size twenty two. I think it's fair to say that you've made my day."

"My pleasure." Jack chuckled. "You'll curse me after a week."

\*\*\*

With care Norma turned the key in the lock, mindful of her mother's afternoon nap. She had an urge to share her good news, and made her way to the front room. Agnes, pale and quiet, lay sprawled face down upon the carpet with her head on a cushion. Norma ran to the prone figure and got down on her knees.

"Mum, are you okay?"

Her mother's eyes flickered open.

"Where have you been? I fell and couldn't get up, so I pulled a cushion off the chair and must have gone to sleep down here. Can you help me up, please?"

*Should she phone and see if Ruth and Gordon were about?* Norma fretted for a few uncertain moments, and then with ease lifted her mother back into her chair.

137

"Thank you." Agnes panted. "The carer had just gone and I got up to find my alarm necklace."

"You should wear it all the time, Mum. What's the use if you have one for emergencies but don't wear it?"

"Oh, I didn't want to bother anybody. I decided I'd just lie here until you came back. Where have you been?"

Some colour had returned to the old lady's cheeks. Norman found his mother's necklace on the dining table and placed it around her neck.

"I've got a little job. I will work in a bar on Friday, Saturday and Sunday lunchtimes. You won't need to cook for me on those days."

"You've got a job?" Agnes replied with some surprise. "A job, did you say?"

"Yes." Norma nodded. "A job."

"Whatever's come over you, Norman?"

"I don't know." Norman shrugged. "I suppose you can say I'm a late developer."

"It seems as though trying to live as a woman has made you come out of your shell a bit."

"Yeah, Mum, I got there in the end. I'm like a tortoise that's been in extra-long hibernation, ha ha."

## Chapter Twenty Seven – Norma

"Two pints, darlin', and one for yourself."

There was more to pouring beer than she had first thought. There was definitely an art to it.

"Cheers. Sorry about the froth. It's my first day."

Seemingly disembodied hands reached out and clutched loose change, notes and bank cards. A sea of faces merged into one another, and she hoped to God she had entered every food order into the computer correctly. Waitresses scurried about with trays, empties piled up on tables, and Jack served customers at the speed of light. Norma wondered whether she had made the biggest mistake of her life.

Melanie appeared at the bar, a vision in sunshine yellow.

"I see Jack's got you working on the chain gang."

"I don't know what I'm doing. I'm so slow. Jack serves five drinks to my one. I haven't even had time to collect the glasses."

"You'll get quicker. I used to slave here until I found permanent work. I'll get some glasses for you, and the girls pick them up anyway. I owe Jack a couple of favours."

"Thanks. You can have the two free drinks I've been offered so far. I haven't had time to think, let alone do anything else."

"One each. You need to drink, or you'll get dehydrated and feel even worse."

Her feet ached after the first hour, and by the end of the shift it was as though she had been run over by a truck. She had never worked so hard in her life. When two o'clock signaled the last of the lunch orders and the end of her first day, Norma flopped down onto the nearest bar stool and exhaled a long sigh.

"Sorry, Jack. I don't think I'm cut out for this."

"Bollocks." Jack grinned. "You've done great. Everyone's slow at first, even Melanie was."

"Cheers, darling." Melanie threw down a basket of empty glasses onto the bar. "I'm working for you for nothing here, *and* I've chipped my nail."

Norma yawned.

"I'm really hungry, but after today I can't face the sight of more scampi and chips."

"Sit there. I'll get you something." Melanie turned towards the kitchen. "Jack, I hope she doesn't have to pay for it."

"Mind your own biz." Jack stuck a middle finger up at Melanie. "Don't use the salmon. That's for tomorrow."

Norma, stupefied, sat on the stool in silence until Melanie placed a chicken superfood salad and cutlery wrapped in a serviette on the bar in front of her.

"Eat up before you fall asleep. Jack says it's free."

"Did I?" Jack replied and stared at Melanie.

"Yeah, you did. Give the poor girl a break."

"I'm so out of shape, Mel." Norma took a knife and fork out of its wrapping. "I need to get fit."

Melanie plonked herself on the next stool.

"Come with me to the gym. You'll either lose some more weight or you'll drop dead from a heart attack."

Norma laughed.

"Oh, I don't know – all that grunting and sweating, and there's the problem when I want to have a shower. Anyway, right now I've got to get through this weekend first."

\*\*\*

She let herself into the house. June's voice shouted from the front room.

"Is that you, Norman?"

"No." Norma raised her voice. "It's Norma!"

Her sister came out into the hallway.

"Blimey, you look knackered. Mum tells me you've got a job?"

"I work in *Jack's Place* along the High Street. I'm the assistant manager."

"Really?" June, surprised, stared at Norma. "You're having me on, right? Oh, I can see your uniform ..."

"I only work at the bar and serve customers. It's a start, but I think I'll like it. Everyone accepts me, just as I am. It helps when you're trying to turn your life around."

"Good for you." June nodded in agreement, "although I'll be the first to say that it's about time. Thanks for your help with Mum the other day when she fell. You should have given me a ring."

"It's down to *me*, I suppose." Norma smiled at her sister. "I live here."

June looked towards the front room and then softened her voice.

"Speaking of living *here*, Steve's organised for the solicitor to come round next Monday evening. I hope you'll still agree that the deeds can be changed to tenants-in-common? Don't forget that we'll then *all* own shares in the house and so it won't be able to be sold for care home fees."

Norma shook her head.

"Whatever you want, but Mum won't need to go into care. I'll keep an eye on her."

She was amused at the sight of her sister's expression.

"Have you had a frontal lobotomy?"

Norma let a snort of laughter escape her lips.

"Not yet, but it might be a good idea, eh?"

"I don't *care* if you change your sex now." June shook her head in wonder. "The new you is a vast improvement on the old one, for sure."

"Thanks." Norma gave June a spontaneous hug. "That's the nicest thing you've ever said to me."

## Chapter Twenty Eight - Ruth

"Missus Wicks, are you happy to change your will so that your house will be owned under the tenants-in-common agreement, and to change ownership via the Land Registry form RX One?"

Ruth looked at her mother, whom she was sure could not hear a single word spoken by the ultra-patient Terrence Kennedy.

"What?"

"Mum!" Ruth moved closer to her mother's ear. "Mister Kennedy wants you to own half of the house and for us to own the other half!"

"Well, isn't that supposed to be why he's here in the first place?" Agnes looked from Ruth to Terrence Kennedy in confusion.

"Missus Wicks," Terrence spoke in a reverential tone, "each tenant will own a share of the property, and each tenant will be able to bequeath their share to whomsoever they wish."

The solicitor waited for an answer. Ruth raised her voice.

"Mum!"

"What?"

"We'll be able to leave our share of the house to anybody we want to, in our wills."

"Yes, I know. Don't shout. I will leave mine to Norman... er ... Norma... so that he has somewhere to live."

"I shall pass mine on to Billy." Steven replied. "What about you, Ruth?"

"Well, we have no children of course." Ruth shrugged. "But I could pass my share on to Billy too, or divide it between Billy and Andrew."

"Thanks." June gave a brief smile. "Andrew will inherit mine. It'll be nice to think the house will be here for the next generation after we're gone."

Terrence Kennedy passed around a sheaf of papers.

"These forms are for you all to sign. You will also need to change your wills and stipulate as to who will benefit from your share of the house upon your death. Tenants-in-common *can* be overridden by a will. If one co-owner wishes to sell then the others can buy him or her out, or he or she is perfectly entitled to sell their share to somebody outside the family."

"I see." Ruth nodded. "So... we'll rely on you to do the paperwork, Mister Kennedy."

"My pleasure." Terrence Kennedy gathered his belongings together. "And for your information my fees at the moment are the same as last year."

\*\*\*

Ruth showed Terrence Kennedy to the door, and then returned to the front room to sit and chat to her mother and siblings. Agnes fell into a light doze. Ruth kicked off her shoes and curled up in one corner of the settee.

"This is like being a kid again – us all here together. We don't often get the chance to meet up now. Norman, who do you think you'll leave your share of the house to?"

Ruth heard a *tut* of irritation from her brother's direction.

"What part of *Norma* do you not understand? I'm *sick* of my wishes being ignored."

"Steady on, Norma." Steven held up one hand. "You've given us a big shock and we've all got to come to terms with it." He turned to Ruth. "Some of us will take longer than others to accept."

Ruth leaned forwards in Steven's direction.

"So Norman's sex change is fine with you?"

"Sure." Steven shrugged. "What can *I* do about it? He – I mean, *she*, will have to live with her decision."

"What if he has his dick chopped off and then changes his mind?"

Ruth caught a flash of anger in Norman's eyes.

"I *won't* change my mind, and I'll certainly *not* leave my share of the house to *you*!"

Ruth raised one corner of her mouth in contempt.

"No, you'll probably leave it to some freak who looks exactly like yourself, and then *he'll* end up owning the majority share."

"Rather him than you."

"Can we talk in a civilized way, perhaps?" June sighed. "Why do we argue about who gets what, while Mum's still alive and kicking? Are we all in agreement that Norman...sorry, I mean *Norma*, can live here once Mum's gone?"

Ruth gave a snort of disapproval.

"No, I *don't* agree, because *he'll* be sitting on our inheritance. Why should *he* end up with all of it if part of the house is in *our* names as well?"

"Probably because we already have houses to live in and Norma hasn't, other than this one." Steven explained with uncommon patience. "Where will she find twenty five thousand quid for a mortgage deposit? She's nearly sixty with no job. She'll never get a mortgage at her age."

"He'll have to rent." Ruth replied with a shrug. "Thousands do."

"But only if they have a job." June interjected. "Norma's buggered as regards somewhere to live if she cannot live *here*."

"You need to get a job, Norman." Ruth hissed. "Enough's enough."

"For your information I *have* got a job. I started last Friday."

"What?" Ruth sat straighter and stared at Norma in surprise.

June piped up with the satisfaction of one who has insider knowledge.

"Yeah, she's Assistant Manager at Jack's Place in the High Street. She loves it."

Norma opened her mouth to speak, she saw June's wink and changed her mind.

"Well done." Ruth replied without conviction. "It's about bloody time. I'll have to go there for lunch one day."

Norma stared at Ruth.

"Please don't."

"Why not?"

"It's a gay bar. You would have much to complain about. After all... people like *me* go there. The place is full of freaks."

Ruth gave an exaggerated sigh.

"I have no prejudice against gay people. What *does* piss me off is lazy people... people that have done bugger all for years and let other people run around after them."

"You just don't understand." Norma shrugged. "You try and work with straight men when you're a male to female transsexual, and then you'll know why I've stayed at home. Try and get a job in an office full of women as well...what a joke *that* is."

"You have to push yourself a little bit harder. Give as good as you get."

Norma stood up.

"Ruth, you talk a load of bollocks."

"That's it... walk away and lock yourself in your room as usual."

"Leave him alone, Ruth." June shook her head. "He's got a point. Sorry… *she's* got a point."

Norma gave a nod of acknowledgement in June's direction.

"Thank you."

## Chapter Twenty Nine - Norma

"Hi. I'm Belinda Smithson."

Norma smiled at a plain-looking woman around forty years of age, slightly overweight, and with thick blonde hair scraped back into a high ponytail.

"Hello. I'm Norma. Am I pleased to see *you*! It's crazy city at lunchtimes just now."

"Yeah, I know. I only work here for a bit of extra money during the summer and autumn. I like it. Jack's a good employer as long as you don't break all the glasses and argue with the customers."

"I've worked here for two weeks." Norma pumped froth from a new barrel of beer. "But I feel as though I've been here all my life."

Belinda nodded.

"It gets you like that. Anyway, don't worry...we can help each other and swap jobs about. As long as everything gets done, then Jack won't mind what we do."

As time went on Norma begun to feel more at home behind the bar. She enjoyed good natured banter with customers, some of whom now had names instead of just faces. In rare quiet moments she watched Belinda's ponytail as her new friend bobbed between tables and collected empties.

"You won't score with that one."

Norma jumped out of her reverie in alarm, her face flushed with the sure and certain knowledge that Jack knew exactly what had been on her mind.

"Eh? What do you mean?"

Jack loaded glasses into the under-counter dishwasher

"Customers know to leave her alone, and that's why she likes to work here. She's asexual."

"Oh." Norma appeared confused. "A sexual *what*?"

Jack roared with laughter.

"Doesn't bat for any side, nor the Middlesex Regiment either come to that."

"Well, I expect that's her business." Norma hid her disappointment. "It's nothing to do with me."

"Sure." Jack nodded. "Just thought I'd pass the word along."

\*\*\*

Was it an accident of birth, nurture or Mother Nature that had first caused her to be attracted to women? Norma had no idea, but she now looked forward to every single weekend and the chance to feast her eyes on Belinda's stocky frame. Mindful of Jack's warning she kept all conversations with Belinda superficial, and was rewarded with an easy-going and pleasant working relationship.

However, by the time summer had turned to autumn, Belinda featured regularly in Norma's tormented dreams. Couples came into the bar and canoodled in corners. Passion went on all around her, and Norma hated the fact that every day she had to fight an unrequited love. *Was it true that some people were actually asexual?* She had no idea, but after three days without sleep she knew that she had to find out whether or not Belinda batted for Middlesex, Sussex, Essex, or all three regiments joined together.

One Saturday afternoon in mid-October the lunchtime clientele had thinned out somewhat. Jack took an early lunch break, Norma wiped the bar clean of beer spillages, and Belinda took clean glasses from the dishwasher and stacked them on a shelf above the till.

"It's my last day tomorrow."

Norma's heart sank.

"Oh. I didn't realise. Where will you work during the winter?"

"Where I work for the rest of the time – at the hospital. I'm a porter...casual work. Sometimes I work mornings and sometimes evenings. It suits me. This is just a bit of extra money."

"I see." Norma nodded. "It's been a pleasure to work with you. I'll miss you."

Belinda smiled.

"I might be back next year. Will Jack keep you on?"

"I don't know." Norma shrugged. "He hasn't said."

"He'll probably let you go, now the summer's coming to an end. Have you got another job?"

Norma shook her head.

"No. This is it for me, but I find I do love to work and feel productive. I spent almost fifty eight years at home on my arse. This year I turned my life around."

"*Wow.*" Belinda looked at Norma in amazement. "Good for you. You should try the hospital. There's often vacancies for porters. I could put in a good word for you if you want? I'm sure you'd get on well there, as you seem a caring sort."

"I've never even considered something like that." Norma had a sudden mental image of wheeling old people about. "Thanks. By the way... would you like to meet up for a drink one evening when you're not at work?"

Belinda chuckled.

"Ah, sorry. I think I'm the only person who works in a bar but doesn't touch alcohol."

A keen disappointment washed over her, but at the same time Norma had an overwhelming urge to check out possible vacancies for NHS porters.

"I don't either, but we could go to the pictures if you like?"

"Sorry." Belinda shook her head. "But thanks for asking."

Norma, bitterly disappointed at her friend's reply, needed to know one thing and one thing only.

"Is it because I'm trans-gender?"

She saw the startled look on Belinda's features and suddenly wished she had kept her mouth shut.

"Oh, no. Please don't take it the wrong way. It's me. I tend to keep to myself. I don't do relationships."

"I wasn't after a relationship." Norma replied as gently as she could. "Just a pleasant evening out."

Embarrassed, Norma wanted the floor to open up so that she could drop out of sight of Belinda, who regarded her in an enigmatic way and carried on emptying the dishwasher in silence.

## Chapter Thirty - Agnes

There was no doubt about it; her son's personality had changed, and indeed had changed for the better. Agnes lifted up the lid of their kitchen bin to find an empty, clean liner. She looked across at the strange spectacle of a bald, middle-aged man with morning stubble on his chin, who sported breasts bigger than hers and ate Weetabix clad in a pink nightdress and matching furry slippers.

"Thanks for taking the rubbish out, Norman...Norma."

"You're welcome."

His voice sounded slightly different, and he had lost a considerable amount of weight. Skin sagged on his upper arms, which before had been firm and muscular. Agnes could not take her eyes off her son. She gripped her trolley and pushed it towards the table.

"Have you taken your Metformin?"

Norma chewed and swallowed a spoonful of cereal before speaking. She nodded.

"They told me at the clinic last week I can start to come off it, so I take it every other day now. I've lost three stones, Mum. My blood sugars are good, and I'll carry on losing more weight."

"What? That's wonderful!" Agnes sat down at the table and lifted a cup of coffee to her lips. "This year has certainly been your year."

"And next year might be even better." Norman chuckled. "I've sent off an application form for a porter's job at the hospital."

Agnes nearly choked on her coffee.

\*\*\*

She knew the three of them would soon fight each other to report in first. Agnes sat close to the phone and wished that she could take it off the hook and concentrate on *Pointless.* June always seemed to ring when *Pointless* was on TV. It occurred to Agnes how *pointless* it was to switch on the television at all. By the time her daughter had finished wittering on, the programme would have finished and then Steven's conversation would spoil the *Six O'clock News.* Ruth would shout over any local news, and so Agnes decided to sit in silence and wait. All she could hear was muted music from the direction of Norman's room.

The phone rang. Agnes pressed the amplification button and put her ear to the receiver.

"Hello June."

Her daughter's throaty chuckle echoed down the line.

"How did you know it was me?"

"I guessed. You always ring first."

"How are you?"

"I'm still alive." Agnes sighed. "How about *you?*"

"Oh, I'm fine. Don't worry about *me.*"

Agnes was sick of nightly banal conversations which interrupted her favourite TV programmes. It was time to put a stop to them.

155

"Is it possible for you all to phone later? Every time I sit down to look at *Pointless*, the phone goes. Perhaps, even better, you can take it in turns so that only *one* of you checks whether I'm still alive every night instead of all three?"

"Sorry, I'm sure."

Her daughter sounded affronted. Agnes pressed a button on the remote control, and Alexander Armstrong's features dominated the TV screen. She wondered whether he would ever decide to wear a tie.

"Ring back around eight o'clock, but no later. I like to have a shower and go to bed at nine."

"Well… it's not always possible if I'm out, but I'll try. I'll tell the others to ring later as well. But hey, you've got Sky TV the same as me. Why don't you press the *pause* button instead and come back to it? It's easy."

"Maybe for you, but I don't know where that is. Norman showed me once, but it never seems to work for me. Anyway, Norman's here if I need him. He even took the rubbish out for the first time today. He's also applied for a porter's job at the hospital."

"Bloody hell." June laughed. "Wonders will never cease. But we need to call him Norma now …it's what he wants. With those boobs he certainly looks more like a woman."

"But he isn't really, is he?" Agnes replied. "He only plays at it."

"You ought to try though, Mum. The more we say *Norma* and *she*, the quicker we'll get used to it."

Agnes wondered whether she would ever watch *Pointless* in its entirety.

"I try all the time, but I'm nearly ninety three. *You* try living for ninety three years and see how long it takes *you* to get used to doing something new."

The line went dead. Agnes turned up the volume on the TV and wished that Richard Osman would buy a new razor.

# Chapter Thirty One - Norma

Dave Metcalf, Estates Manager at Fulham General Hospital, regarded the capable–looking person in front of him.

"Well Norma…sorry about the three weeks we've taken to contact you. We had quite a few interviews to do. I see you've worked in a bar for the past few months."

"Yes, that's right, but it was just a summer job." Norma nodded in agreement. "Did Jack Metcalf send in a reference for me?"

"He did." Dave looked at a piece of headed paper. "You'll be pleased to hear he says you're a good, reliable worker. Um … how come this had been your only job in forty years?"

Norma grimaced.

"It's a long story. This year I've come out as transgender, and identifying as a woman has made me happy. I sat at home, confused and angry for years until I decided not to take the easy option anymore. I guess I live true to myself now, and I'm trying hard to change my life around."

Dave perused the CV in front of him for a moment.

"Good for you. It must take guts to do what you've done."

Norma shrugged.

"Jack gave me a chance to prove myself. There's somebody else here who you can speak to about me... Belinda Smithson. She's a friend of mine. I think she might have mentioned me to you?"

She was aware of a strange shift in atmosphere at the mention of Belinda's name. Dave kept his eyes fixed on a sheaf of papers piled high on his desk.

"Yes, I believe she did. What are you able to do as regards shift work?"

"I have no commitments." Norma ignored the change of subject. "I can work any shift. I'm currently on Job Seeker's Allowance, but if I can work full time then of course I'll stop the benefit. Other than that I can work up to sixteen hours a week and still keep it."

"You realise that being a porter means that sometimes you will be asked to transport deceased patients to the mortuary. How do you feel about that?"

"I'll be truthful. I guess I don't know because I've never done it." Norma managed to conceal her surprise. "But hey, they can't hurt me if they're dead, can they? I'm sure I'll get used to it."

Dave nodded and sat back in his chair.

"What do you think are your strengths and weaknesses?"

Norma laughed.

"I've just lost three stones in weight, and changed from male to female, and so you could say I'm a very determined person once I set my mind to something. As for weaknesses, well... I suppose I haven't socialised much, although working for Jack Metcalf *made* me talk to people. I've missed out on a lot of life while I sat in my bedroom. I want to do something about it now."

"Great." Dave jotted down a few more notes. "Another question for you... if you saw a confused elderly person wandering around the hospital corridors in their pajamas, what would you do?"

Norma wracked her brain, and quelled the urge to panic under the pressure to provide a correct answer.

"I don't know *this* hospital's system, but I remember when I stayed in hospital as a child to have my tonsils out I had to wear some kind of name tag on my wrist. I didn't want to wear it and tried to pull it off. I assume this elderly person would also wear a name tag and perhaps it would state the ward they were on too? If I couldn't see a ward name on it, then I'd take the person to the nearest ward and hope the nurses could find them and where they were supposed to be on whatever computer system they have."

"And when could you start?"

"Oh, anytime." Norma held up the palms of both hands. "Anytime at all."

Dave stood up and held out his right hand.

"Thanks for coming along today. I have just three more people to interview. You'll hear from us soon."

Norma shook Dave's hand and hoped for the best. As she walked back along the corridor to the main entrance she looked out for Belinda, but her friend was nowhere in sight.

\*\*\*

She combed her wig on its stand and listened for the postman. Today, just to spite her, he was late. Norma stood up and walked over to the window. A red Royal Mail van had parked further along the street and the postman scuttled between bungalows, arms filled with letters and parcels. Norma fitted the wig back on her head, and made her way out of the front door and along the garden path.

"Anything for number thirty six?"

Did she sense the postman's unease at the sight of her, or was she just paranoid? Norma took two letters; one for her mother, and one addressed to herself which showed Fulham General Hospital's franking stamp. She ripped open the envelope and screamed out loud as she learned the start date for her new life as a trainee hospital porter.

## Chapter Thirty Two - Norma

Norma, shy and awkward on her first day as a hospital porter, sensed Dave's unease as he pointed out both male and female changing rooms. There and then she decided to go back home before she took any showers, and to use an individual unisex toilet or a disabled toilet rather than cause any embarrassment amongst her colleagues.

Most of that initial day was spent in the classroom, with Moving and Handling, Fire Training, and Conflict Resolution courses to digest, along with a map in order to learn the layout of the hospital. Her head swam with new information.

On her third day at a welcome tea break she looked around the staff quarters for a sighting of Belinda, but she assumed her friend had another off-duty day or annual leave. When the last induction course had ended she wandered back to the staff room to say goodbye. Just one porter, Jimmy Lester, a volunteer well past retirement age, sat in the most comfortable armchair with a newspaper and sipped his tea. Norma collected her jacket and gave Jimmy a wave.

"Sorry I haven't been of much use yet, Jimmy. I've been on various courses. Tomorrow will be different."

Jimmy nodded and turned a page.

"Don't worry, we all had to do them. If you're anything like me I came out and didn't remember a thing."

"That's about it, I'm afraid." Norma laughed. "Er... do you know when Belinda will be next in, by the way?"

"You mean *our* Belinda?" Jimmy looked up. "Belinda Smithson?"

"Yes. Belinda put in a good word for me and I'm sure it was because of her I got this job, but I haven't seen her about."

Jimmy scratched his head and appeared ill at ease.

"No-one's told you then?"

Norma's heart danced a sudden tattoo in her chest.

"Told me *what*?"

"That she checked out last week. Topped herself. *Brown bread*, mate. Her mother came in and told us last Friday."

Norma wondered if she had heard right. Her head whirled and she sat down in haste.

"Are you all right?" Jimmy regarded Norma with concern. "You've gone a bit peaky."

Norma struggled to contain her emotions and speak at the same time.

"I –I didn't know. I did bar work with her in the summer. She never gave any indication that she was suicidal."

"Nor to us." Jimmy shook his head. "So young. Her funeral's in a fortnight if you want to come along. A couple of us porters will go, and some of her friends from other departments."

"Thank you." Norma wiped her eyes and blew her nose. "Yes, I *will* go. Can I sit here a minute? I just can't believe it."

"I'll make you a cup of char." Jimmy stood up. "It gave *us* a bit of a shock as well."

The tea arrived sweeter than she was used to, but Norma drank it down and was grateful. On a more even keel, she turned to Jimmy.

"Did Belinda leave a note?"

"Don't think so." Jimmy shrugged. "But then again her old lady didn't say. You never know just what goes on in people's heads, do you?"

"She was just so... *alive*." Norma sighed. "It doesn't seem possible."

Two other porters returned at the end of their shift; Errol, a cheerful Jamaican, and Mario, slight in stature and with a wiry physique. Norma, thankful that neither man showed her any attention apart from a cursory glance, walked over to the sink and washed up her cup.

"I'll see you all tomorrow." She picked up her belongings and made for the door. "Thanks for the tea, Jimmy."

"Get a good night's kip." Jimmy gave her a wave. "You'll need it."

## Chapter Thirty Three - Norma

Her legs ached after two hours of pounding the hospital corridors, and Norma wondered whether she would be able to last out until the end of her first week. There were patients to wheel from various wards to the X-Ray Department, to the MRI scanner, and to several outpatient clinics dotted around the hospital grounds, and there were swabs and samples to take to Pathology. She dreaded the call to 'Rose Cottage' and its cold steel slabs, but so far on her first morning all patients had remained alive.

For once in her life she felt useful. For nigh on sixty years she had been cocooned in her bedroom, afraid to face the world as a woman. As far as she could tell, some patients seemed far worse off than she was, and they were all grateful for her help. Norma forced herself to cease her search for Belinda in the corridors. She was so busy that she found she could put her own troubles aside and concentrate on trying to brighten somebody's day.

She copied Jimmy and kept her walkie-talkie clipped to her shirt. It seemed that as soon as she had dropped one patient off somewhere, then there was another one who wanted to be picked up. There were also beds to be moved, stationery to take to secretaries, and the post to sort and deliver twice a day.

At twelve o'clock, Norma, grateful for a lunch break, sank down into an armchair in the porters' staff room. One by one her colleagues filed in, made a hot drink and opened up lunch boxes. She lowered her head and looked at her phone, awkward and shy in a place where everybody knew everybody else. Grateful that Jimmy came to sit next to her, Norma bit into a ham and tomato wrap and looked up with a smile. Jimmy's endearing Cockney accent reminded her of her long-deceased grandparents.

"The old pins playing up yet?"

She laughed.

"You could say that. I think I've walked a few miles this morning.

"It's usual to walk about ten by the end of the day." Jimmy took a noisy gulp of tea. "It keeps me going. I'm seventy two, you know. Fit as a butcher's dog."

"Really?" Norma gave Jimmy a more than cursory glance. "Well...I live in hope that I'll lose even more weight doing this job."

Errol Reed opened up a box of sandwiches.

"I've lost four stones. Man, I've never been so healthy."

"I never put on any weight." Mario patted his stomach. "No matter how much pasta I eat."

"I've got to just over three stones gone." Norma nodded. "I used to have diabetes, but now I don't need to take any more tablets."

"Yeah, same here." Errol agreed. "If I hadn't had this job I'd probably be dead by now."

Bill Kirk entered the staff room; slow, stolidly built, and already chewing on a chocolate bar.

"I can eat anything I like and never put on an ounce, just as long as I don't swallow it."

Norma chuckled and stretched out her legs to rest.

"All this walking's no good for me plates though." Jimmy yawned. "Still, mustn't grumble."

"What plates?" Errol appeared confused. "You've got a plastic lunchbox."

"Bunions." Jimmy rolled his eyes to the heavens. "It doesn't do my feet any good."

Errol shook his head in confusion.

"Speak English, man."

"I *am*." Jimmy laughed. "Norma knows what I'm on about, don't you?"

"Only because my grandparents were Cockneys. You remind me of my grandad."

"Glad to be of service." Jimmy replied. "We'll teach Errol and Mario some slang, eh?"

Errol roared with laughter.

"Weh yuh ah seh?"

"Eh?"

Norma laughed, and by the time she had met porters Keith and Eddie her lunch hour was up and she was much more at home.

\*\*\*

She felt as though she had run a marathon. Norma unlocked the front door and with a grateful sigh hung up her jacket and bag.

"Hi Mum, I'm home!"

She could hear Ruth's strident tones. Norma, dismayed, took off her shoes and padded into the front room. Her sister looked up.

"*There* you are. Will you leave Mum on her own *every* day then?"

"I've got a job." Norma gave Ruth an icy stare. "You've told me to get one for years. Now I have. No reason why *you* can't sit with Mum."

"I don't need anybody to sit with me." Agnes regarded Ruth and Norma with contempt. "I'm not a baby."

Ruth ignored Agnes and directed her gaze towards Norma.

"*I* don't live here. *You* have been waited on hand and foot for years. It's about time *you* looked after Mum."

Norma yawned, sat in an armchair, and put her feet on a stool."

"*You* work, and so why shouldn't I? Mum can always ring me on my mobile phone if she's in trouble."

"Huh." Ruth snorted. "You never answer it."

"That's because it's usually always one of you lot. You nag and shout at me all the time, and it pisses me off. If Mum rings when I'm at work, then I'll answer it now."

Norma wondered why her sister was always so angry. She looked across at her mother, frail and tired. The old lady, at some loss to hear what was going on, looked confused and very similar to Edith Parry whom she had trundled along in a wheelchair to have an x-ray not two hours before. She raised her voice.

"Would you like me to do anything, Mum?"

"No." Agnes shook her head. "I'll get dinner in a minute."

Ruth rolled her eyes.

"*Now* he asks! It's only taken him fifty seven years!"

"I'm a *she*." Norma sighed. "How many more times have I got to tell you?"

Ruth snorted in derision.

"What *she* has a *dick*? I don't know of any... do you?"

Once again Norma decided to remove herself from the cause of such conflict. She stood up, took a deep breath, and walked to her room as sedately as she could manage.

\*\*\*

Her mother's voice pierced her dream. Norma woke up to the sight of Agnes gripping her trolley.

"She's gone. Come on, I've cooked some dinner."

The power nap had left her refreshed. Norma swung her legs over the side of the bed and stood up.

"Sorry. I had to get away before I bopped her one."

"I've had a lot of time today to sit and think. "Agnes turned the trolley around with some effort. "I'm very proud of you for what you've achieved. Ruth's wrong, you know."

Norma looked at her mother.

"About what?"

"That you're not a woman. I've never seen you so determined. You're as much of a woman as she is."

Norma, determined not to cry in front of her mother, followed the old lady into the kitchen.

"I'll wash up afterwards." She gave her mother a hug. "And then I'll take the rubbish out."

Exercise had made her ravenous. Norma wolfed down chicken, pasta and vegetables in record time. She noticed how her mother watched her with half a smile.

"It's good for my old eyes to see such a change in you."

"Mum, I've always been the odd one out, the misfit. Now I'm not anymore."

"None of us in our wildest dreams ever thought something like this would happen to *you*, of all people."

"I thought it *might* happen one day." Norma chuckled. "But I had no idea *when* until recently, when I couldn't wait any longer. Sorry I've upset the apple cart."

"No, not at all." Agnes shook her head. "To be honest, I think you're quite remarkable to have come out like this. We'll get used to it. Just give us time."

## Chapter Thirty Four - Norma

She was pleased with the fit of the new black suit. The skirt, now size sixteen, was not even tight. The jacket stretched adequately across her breasts, and a crisp white blouse completed the ensemble. Norma adjusted her wig, and pulled on a pair of black tights and a pair of black court shoes. The florist had delivered a wicker basket of carefully arranged lilies. She picked up the basket, then walked into the front room where her mother sat and read a morning newspaper.

"I've got a few hours off work to attend Belinda's funeral. Errol will drive us all there in a minibus. I'll come back and change afterwards and then return to the hospital. Phone if you need me."

"I'm all right, Norma." Agnes nodded. "Don't you worry about *me*."

Outside she could hear Errol as he sounded his horn. The scent from the lilies was overpowering. Norma tried to keep her fear in check in the knowledge that she had never attended a funeral, not even her father's; once again she had taken the easy option all those years ago and copped out.

From the driver's seat Errol held up one arm in acknowledgement as she walked along the garden path. Bill slid the side door of the minibus across, and Norma climbed in. Most of the seats were taken by people from other departments. She sat next to Bill as Errol pulled away from the kerb. Jimmy waved from across the aisle.

"I didn't realise there were so many people going." Norma exhaled a shaky breath. "She was very popular."

"Everyone liked Belinda." Bill unwrapped a chocolate and popped it into his mouth. "She always brought a ray of sunshine with her. Keith and Eddie wanted to go too, but they had morning shifts."

Chatter ceased as the bus approached the crematorium. Norma's heart raced as she climbed down the steps of the minibus. A member of the crematorium staff ushered the group into a side room to await the arrival of the undertakers.

Norma had no idea what to say; even Jimmy was subdued. She stood by a window until a shiny black hearse carrying Belinda's flower-bedecked coffin came to a halt outside, accompanied by two dark limousines. She followed her work colleagues into the crematorium, and took a seat near the back. Soothing piped music played over a PA system. The backs of two women's blonde heads were visible in the front row, the older woman wept, and the younger one sat stoically upright.

The non-religious service surprised Norma. She listened as a celebrant read a eulogy written by her friend's sister. Both women in the front row now clutched each other for support, and the two blonde heads merged as one as other members of the family stood at the dais to speak.

172

Norma approved of Belinda's three choices of music; Dream Theater's 'The Spirit Lives On', Andrea Bocelli and Sarah Brightman's duet 'Time to Say Goodbye', and Frank Sinatra's rendition of 'It was a Very Good Year'. When at length the coffin traversed through thick velvet curtains there was hardly a dry eye left amongst the congregation. Norma saw a startling family resemblance as the two chief mourners led the congregation outside where wreaths and huge bouquets of flowers laid on the concrete beside a plaque which bore Belinda's name.

Norma made it a point to stand beside Belinda's sister, who stared with unseeing eyes at the many flower arrangements.

"She was my only friend." Norma whispered. "Your sister helped me to get a job at the hospital. Why ever didn't she say she was unhappy? Lovely eulogy, by the way. Sorry… I don't know your name."

The blonde haired woman, an older almost carbon copy of Belinda, turned towards Norma.

"Bernadette, but I'm known as *Bernie*. My sister was a very private person. Nobody knew her really, not even me or Mum."

"Pleased to meet you, Bernie." Norma sniffed. "I first met her when we worked at Jack's Place. We got on like a house on fire."

"Are you Norma?" Bernie asked with interest. "Belinda sometimes mentioned your name when we spoke on the phone."

"I am." Norma nodded. "I still can't believe she's gone."

"Me either." Bernie gave a sigh. "It's nice to find somebody who Belinda got on well with. If you like, you can come back to the house. There's a family lunch laid out, and tea and coffee, but you're very welcome."

"I would, but I've got to go back to work." Norma grimaced. "Sorry."

"Come round after your shift, then." Bernie laid a hand briefly on Norma's arm. "I'm sure Mum would love to meet you. Sixty four Tweed Street."

"I know that road. It's not too far from us." Norma nodded. "My brother fell off his bike there when he was about fifteen and broke his arm."

Bernie picked up a wreath and read the attached card.

"We'll be able to talk about Belinda. Perhaps we can figure out exactly why she took all those tablets."

## Chapter Thirty Five - Bernie

Bernie opened the front door to an obvious transgender woman. However, her philosophy had always been to live and let live and to walk a mile in someone else's shoes before she made a judgement.

"Come in, Norma. Have you had some dinner?"

"Yes, thanks. Mum had cooked a chicken curry. Sorry I'm a bit late."

"No problem. I'll put the kettle on."

It seemed strange to be back in her childhood home again. Her mother, Sonia, usually so distant and self-reliant, had begged her to stay just one more night. Bernie had railed against becoming Sonia's only support, and already the tendrils of emotional blackmail had threatened to engulf her.

She brought Norma into the front room.

"Mum, this is Norma. She was at the funeral today and was a friend of Belinda's. Norma, meet my mum Sonia."

"Hi." Norma smiled at an elderly woman sitting in an armchair. "Pleased to meet you."

Sonia Smithson, tired and wrung out with grief, wondered if the unusual looking woman in front of her was the reason for her daughter's death.

"Sorry, I didn't really notice anybody today."

"That's okay." Norma replied. "I stayed at the back and didn't really want to intrude."

"Do sit down and tell me how you knew my daughter, while Bernie makes some tea."

Bernie hoped that Norma was not in for a full inquisition. She willed the kettle to come to the boil, and flung three cups on a tray with some milk, sugar and biscuits. She hated all the fuss her mother made with a teapot, but knew she would complain if the tea was not brewed to her preferred consistency. She squeezed the full teapot in-between the cups and in haste made her way back along the hallway. She heard Norma's voice as she opened the door.

"I didn't know her *that* well. She hardly ever talked about her personal life. We just worked together, that's all."

"Help yourself." Bernie put the tray down in front of Norma. "Biscuits if you like."

Norma raised her right thumb.

"Thanks. I know you're looking for answers as to why Belinda took her own life, but I don't think I can add anything to what you already know."

Sonia poured some tea into a cup and added some milk.

"Were you two an item?"

"Sorry?"

Bernie gave her mother a hard stare.

"Mum …what a thing to ask!"

"It's a perfectly reasonable request." Sonia sighed. "I just need to know. You see, I think my daughter might have been gay, but she, well, you know, never came out and said it."

Bernie wished her mother would shut up. Norma appeared crestfallen.

"No, we weren't an item, but if she had come out, things might have ended differently. You see, I'm gay too. I did ask her whether she wanted to go to the cinema or come out for drink one time, but she said no. Jack Metcalf at the pub didn't think she was attracted to men *or* women. Perhaps *that* was the problem."

"I see." Sonia, gloomy, drained her cup. "I just want to get to the bottom of why she did this. She left no note."

Bernie sighed.

"Mum, I don't think we'll *ever* find out. Sure, she was tormented by *something*, but she wanted to keep it to herself and so we have to move on."

"I suppose so." Sonia agreed. "Look, I'm tired, and it's been a long day. I'm going up for a bath and then to bed. It was nice to meet you, Norma, but I'll leave you with Bernie for now."

Norma nodded.

"Sorry I couldn't be of more help."

Bernie waited until her mother had left the room and then sat back in her chair.

"*Phew.* Sorry about Mum. We wondered if you might have had some more information."

She caught Norma making a surreptitious scope of the room.

"'Fraid not. Was there anybody special in her life? Was she ever married?"

"No, and no." Bernie shook her head. "I guess she was a little odd in that way. She didn't even bring a friend home for tea when she was at school."

"Huh, she sounds just like me." Norma chuckled. "That's because I never went to school much, and so didn't have any."

"Seems like you and Belinda might have had a lot in common. Shame you both got going a bit late."

Norma shrugged.

"Story of my life."

"I reckon we could both do with a drink." Bernie stood up. "What say we go to Jack's Place? I haven't lived around here for years, and I'd like to see where Belinda worked."

"Okay, but it's a gay bar. Are you all right with that?"

"I'm bi, so sure." Bernie laughed. "Whatever. Come on, let's go."

\*\*\*

She liked the way that nobody took any notice of them. Bernie followed Norma to the bar and plonked herself down on a stool. A man dressed in vivid purple made his way towards them.

"What are you doing here, Norma? I only ever see you at lunchtimes."

Bernie noticed how Norma seemed quite at ease in their surroundings.

"Hi Jack. It's been a long day. This is Belinda's sister, Bernie."

Bernie held out her hand, aware of the man's scrutiny.

"Hey Jack."

"Enchanted." Jack held her hand in a soft grip. "You look very much like your sister. I heard through the grapevine what had happened."

Bernie nodded.

"I decided to come along and see where she worked. She liked it here. I usually live up north, but I'm down here with my mum for a few days."

"Yeah, she got on well here." Jack replied. "She was a bit of a loner, and she liked it that people left her alone. I did try it on with her once, *anyone's* fair game as far as I'm concerned, but she told me to fuck off."

Bernie laughed.

"That sounds like Belinda."

"Can I buy you two ladies a drink?" Jack looked from Bernie to Norma. "Gin's on special offer tonight."

"Yea, go on then...gin and tonic for me please." Bernie raised her right thumb. "What about you, Norma?"

"Lemonade for me. I don't drink."

"A very sensible lady." Jack nodded. "One lemonade and a G and T coming up."

Bernie swiveled around in her stool towards Norma.

"Why don't you drink?"

She was surprised at Norma's reply.

"Why do *you*?"

"Fair enough." Bernie laughed. "Sorry. I was just being nosey."

"No, *I'm* sorry." Norma sighed. "I'm so used to hiding the real me under Norman's shield. I need to be more open, I know. I don't drink alcohol because it's never mixed with Metformin, and anyway, to tell you the truth I don't think I could bear to be out of control of my senses."

"Oh, I see. Bernie nodded. "One of *those*. You don't know what you've missed. It's rather nice. You just don't *care*."

"*I* would care." Norma laughed. "Strange… I've never told anybody that before. You've winkled it out of me."

Bernie smiled. She could see why her sister had liked this unusual lady-man. She was also aware of a longer-than-usual eye contact. Was there a spark of interest behind Norma's high, protective wall?

"I think I might stay for a few more days and help Mum out. She's got so much paperwork to sort out, and she's still in a bit of a state. Perhaps we can meet up again and talk about Belinda?"

"Sure." Norma nodded in agreement. "It'll be good for both of us."

## Chapter Thirty Six - Ruth

Evening Bridge Club now forgotten, Ruth paced the front room carpet and wished June had answered her mother's call for help instead.

"Where's Norman gone now, Mum? Shouldn't he be *here* when he finishes work to look after you?"

A familiar wave of anger flashed over her at the mention of her brother's name. It was really too bad of him to go out every evening and leave their mother alone.

"He's got a friend at last, but I don't think she lives round here." Agnes shrugged. "I don't mind. A nice girl came round last night, and then they went off to the pictures. She had a boy's name, but I can't remember what it was. I don't blame Norman for trying to have a bit of a life."

Ruth rolled her eyes.

"He's nearly sixty, for Christ's sake. He's left all this sex change thing a bit late, don't you think?"

"Well, at least he's got something going for him now." Agnes chuckled. "It's not normal to sit in your bedroom day after day. Sorry to call you out. I couldn't lift the saucepan of water. Norman usually does it."

Ruth sighed.

"Mum, you need to go into a home. You're ninety two. If Norman's going to be out all the time, then you'll have a bit of a problem."

"I *am* in a home." Agnes shook her head. "My own one. Wait until *you're* ninety two and see if *you* want to sit in a room all day with a load of smelly old people."

"But if Norman's not around, how will you manage? Gordon and I go to work all day, and so do Steve and June. You fall about and can't lift things, can't do this and can't do that. How can I keep running round here all the time? It's not always convenient, you know."

Her mother sat stubbornly silent. Ruth wanted to scream with frustration.

\*\*\*

"It's eleven o'clock at night. I've waited here for hours for you to come in. Mum had an emergency, and you left her here on her own."

Ruth spat out the torrent of words as her tension lifted. To her annoyance her brother just shrugged his shoulders and hung up his coat in the hallway.

"What emergency? She's in *bed*."

"She couldn't lift a saucepan of potatoes to drain them. You had gone out."

"I'd hardly call that an emergency." Norma yawned. "Why didn't she lift them out with a spoon?"

"Because for eighty odd years she's poured them into a colander to drain. Try and tell her to change the habits of a lifetime."

Norman turned around and walked towards his room.

"Well, *you* go out to *your* various clubs. *You* have a social life, and now *I* want one too. Is that too much to ask? Mum will have to change her way of doing things if she won't go into a care home and I'm out for the evening. I'm here to help her in the mornings when she gets up. Perhaps you, June and Steve need to take it in turns to be here in the evenings? If not, then I'll end up being as much a prisoner in here as I've always been. I don't think it's fair that I should do it all."

"But all these years you've done sod all!" Ruth's voice rose as she followed behind him. "You've laid on your bed and let Mum do *everything*."

"Yeah, I *was* fat and lazy." Norma turned to face her. "But now I'm who I want to be, I'm happy, and I want to turn my life around. Have you seen how much weight I've lost? In a few more weeks I'd have got rid of four stones of blubber. I *do* help Mum now, but I also need a life of my own, just like *you* have."

She was tired and could not argue the toss with him anymore. Ruth stormed back to the hallway, picked up her bag and coat, and opened the front door. A cool breeze fanned her burning cheeks, and an owl hooted from a nearby tree. All was quiet. She closed the door and pressed a button on her keyring to turn off the car's central locking system. When she pulled away from the kerb she looked over her shoulder, and her brother, wigless, stared balefully out at her from his front bedroom window.

## Chapter Thirty Seven - Norma

"Somerset ward. Bay four, bed two. One for Rose Cottage."

"Right."

Norma replaced the receiver with a heavy heart. Just her and Jimmy were in-between jobs, and she knew the manager of Somerset ward would want the unfortunate corpse out of the way and the bed disinfected as soon as possible.

"Jimmy. There's a patient for Rose Cottage."

"Come on then." Jimmy stood up. "First one for you?"

Norma nodded.

"Yeah. I guess it'd happen sooner or later."

"Nothing to it." Jimmy shrugged. "The body will be wrapped in a sheet. All we have to do is lift it onto a trolley and take it to the mortuary attendant. Easy peasy."

"Okay."

Full of trepidation, Norma pulled out a body trolley and cover from the storage unit and with Jimmy on the other end, pushed it along the corridor to Somerset ward. Even though it was only mid-day, all the curtains around the beds were closed. Norma checked in with the ward clerk at the desk, and then followed Jimmy to Bay four.

Behind the screen a tiny form lay wrapped from head to toe in a sheet. An identity label had been stuck on the patient's abdomen, and another tied to one foot. Norma manoeuvered herself to stand at the deceased patient's feet, and in sorrow read part of the label: *'Ada Reeves, aged 92'*.

At that precise moment Norma imagined her mother, of a similar age, ending up in the same undignified state. She mused on how short life was. Indeed, more than half of her own life had already slipped away, and she had to face the inevitability that her mother's time on earth would soon be done.

"We'll lift on *three*."

She came out of her reverie with a start and nodded to Jimmy.

"One... two... *three*."

Ada, light as a feather, offered no resistance. With the plastic cover in place, Norma and Jimmy took Ada along the back corridor and rang the mortuary bell. A tall young man who chewed gum pointed to an empty fridge.

"In there."

Norma stared down at her hands and pulled out the fridge's sliding drawer. It could have been her own mother on the slab. Somebody, somewhere had lost a wife, a mum, a grandmother, a sister, or an aunt.

\*\*\*

"Can I do anything to help you?"

Norma noticed the look of surprise on her mother's face.

"*You*... do something to help *me*?"

The heavy sarcasm was not lost on Norma. However, instead of her usual acidic response, she stood her ground and forced her features to crack into a grimace. She raised her voice to accommodate ancient ears.

"I'll take the rubbish out, and then I'll have a hoover round. You won't need to get another cleaner. I'll do it."

She wanted to laugh at her mother's expression; the old lady's mouth had formed an 'o' of surprise.

"This is all very nice, and I'm pleased to say it happens more and more." Agnes looked at Norma in confusion. "But what's brought it all on?"

Norma gave a slight grimace.

"For years I sat in my room and raged against the world. Everyone but me was sure of their gender. Life made me angry but I've sorted myself out and I'm a lot happier now. My life will be complete when I've had the gender reassignment surgery, and believe me, Mum, I *will* have it."

She waited for her mother's reaction.

"I'm sure you will, Norma. You seem altogether a different person."

"That's because I *am*."

She had hated her mother and sisters because they were female, but now there was a growing kinship with June. To her delight even her mother and Steve could see how she had changed. There was just one more battle to be fought.

*Ruth.*

186

## Chapter Thirty Eight - Agnes

The telephone rang just as *Pointless* came on screen. Agnes turned up the speaker's volume and knew that if she'd had the strength she would have yanked the cord out of the wall and thrown the phone, receiver and all, out the window.

"Yes?"

"It's Ruth. How are you?"

"I was just about to watch *Pointless*, and then *you* rang."

"Well...excuse me for living!"

Her daughter's voice had already started to rise. Agnes decided it was time to change the subject"

"Norman really surprised me yesterday."

"Yeah?" Ruth answered with interest. "How?"

"He... I mean, *she*... dusted, hoovered, washed up the dishes and took the rubbish out ...*again*."

Ruth let out a snort of laughter.

"Blimey ...what's he up to?"

"Nothing, as far as I can tell. He's turned over a new leaf."

"Let me speak to him." Ruth chuckled. "Put him on."

"He...*she's* not here. She's gone out with her friend."

Agnes could hear Ruth as she exhaled with force on the other end.

"What? A friend? Male or female?"

"Female I think, and her name's Bernie." Agnes turned up the speaker volume. "All I'm glad is that she's got one at last."

"He's left you home alone again?"

Agnes sighed.

"I'm not a baby. I don't need looking after. I can get in and out of my new chair, and I've got Pointless to watch on TV just as long as the phone doesn't keep ringing."

"Hint taken." Ruth laughed. "I'll pop round tomorrow and have a look at the new Norman. Tell him not to go out."

"*Her.*" Agnes stated. "He doesn't like it otherwise."

"Well, *you* just said *he* doesn't like it."

Agnes gave a *tut* of annoyance.

"Oh God, I don't think I'll ever come to terms with this. I'm so used to the fact that he's always been a man."

She put the phone down, annoyed that she had missed the start of her programme again. Next time she would take it off the hook and everyone would have to bloody well wait.

\*\*\*

Agnes hid a faint annoyance as she listened to Ruth, seemingly still offended by the new normal Norma.

"She won't leave the house to *you*, you know. She'll leave it to all of us."

"I'm not dead yet." Agnes stared at Ruth. "I'm still here… in this room."

Norma shrugged.

"I don't want any more than my share."

"So why the little housekeeper all of a sudden?" Ruth regarded Norma with suspicion. "If not for that?"

"Because I'm living true to myself and I'm happy about it."

Agnes looked from one daughter to the other.

"Will you two pack it in? Ruth, accept that your brother is now your sister and let's move on."

Ruth gave a haughty sniff.

"Well… I must say, the new Norma is better than the old Norman. At least he's not a lazy git anymore."

"*She.*" Agnes stated once more for her daughter's benefit. "The *he* is a *she.*"

Ruth let out a roar of laughter.

"She's walked on the wild side! Has she shaved her legs and plucked her eyebrows?"

"Of course." Norma nodded. "Haven't *you*? At least you haven't got to shave your chest hair as well. I'm a woman now, so bloody well hurry up and accept it."

Agnes hadn't had so much entertainment since the previous night's *Pointless*.

"What wild side?" She looked at Ruth. "Why is it wild to shave your legs and pluck your eyebrows?"

Ruth rolled her eyes.

"I'm talking about Lou Reed."

"Who's she?" Agnes, confused looked from Ruth to Norma. "Does *she* do it then?"

Norma and Ruth looked at one another and burst into giggles.

"Ah well, she's a *he*." Norma giggled. "But he wrote a song about a *he* changing to a *she*."

Agnes closed her eyes and laid her head on the back of the chair.

"I don't know what the matter is with people today. Really, I don't. I think they're all on drugs."

## Chapter Thirty Nine - Bernie

She had looked forward to the evening ahead, and had hopefully dressed to impress. As they sat on bar stools in *Jack's Place* and chatted, Bernie wondered if her sister had enjoyed Norma's company as much as she did herself.

"And so did Ruth say anything else to you last night after your mother had fallen asleep?"

Norma took a sip of cola and nodded.

"Yeah, funnily enough, she did. She said she hopes it all works out for me okay. She seemed quite *human* last night. I think she has grudgingly accepted me as I am."

"Well, that's great." Bernie stated with enthusiasm. "So what's next on the agenda for the new Norma?"

"Oh... I don't know." Norma shrugged. "I'm happy with things as they are at the moment. I'm still not used to going out to work and being a woman."

Bernie waggled a finger in Norma's direction.

"A romance. That's what you need. A little bit of love action."

"Who the hell would fancy *me*?" Norma giggled. "I mean... under the wig I'm bald, and under the dress, well... what's *under* the dress doesn't go with what's *over* the dress."

"I think you've got a great personality. You shouldn't put yourself down like that."

"I'm not looking for love." Norma gave a smile. "Enough has happened to me this year without a romance to complicate things even further, and to be honest, I've recently decided that I want to have my surgery first. I need to be a whole woman, if you know what I mean. Hey, let's face it, I'm not the fanciable type." Norma chuckled. "The oestrogen treatment kills your libido for starters. At the moment I'm happy with a book and a cup of cocoa before bed. I've got a face that only a mother could love."

Bernie giggled.

"I'm bi, as you know. I don't care what gender *anyone* is. I just enjoy the sex. Real uncomplicated stuff."

"Good for you." Norma stared at the menu. "Have you got a partner?"

"Yeah, well…sort of, but nothing serious. He lives in Durham, sometimes with me and sometimes not. We're an item, but we see other people as well."

"Oh, right."

Bernie saw Norma's expression register slight dismay, and she wondered whether she had given her new friend too much information.

"I think if I ever had a *significant other*, then I'd want them to be faithful." Norma raised one hand towards Jack and lifted her empty glass. "It's the sort of person I am. I'd be loyal, and I'd expect my partner to be the same. I'd like something along the lines that my grandparents had. They were married for fifty years and only had eyes for each other."

"I think that's a pipe dream these days." Bernie shrugged. "No-one's faithful anymore. It's just the way it is."

Norma shook her head.

"*I* would be. Perhaps I'm the exception to the rule. When you live with a life partner or get married, you're supposed to stay monogamous. What's the point otherwise?"

Bernie had never met anybody quite like the man-woman who sat next to her. More intrigued than ever, she tried to imagine staying faithful to one partner for the rest of her life. The idea had never even occurred to her.

"Not being funny, but you do have a kind of roses-round-the-door dream of a perfect love. Life just isn't like that."

"Then I'll carry on with my book and cocoa." Norma stated with conviction. "I want to be loved for *me*, and not just for sex."

"You do sound remarkably like a woman though." Bernie laughed. "Congratulations."

Norma giggled and Bernie enjoyed the camaraderie. So far the evening had gone well.

\*\*\*

Bernie walked in silence with Norma to her garden gate.

"I won't ask you in. Mum will be in bed, and I've got to get up for an early shift at the hospital tomorrow."

"That's absolutely fine." Bernie nodded in agreement. "I've enjoyed chatting to you tonight. Hopefully we can do this again before I go back?"

Norma smiled.

"Of course. It's a novelty for me to be out and about at night. I like it."

Bernie gave a final wave and carried on walking. She mulled over the evening as she pounded the pavements. *Was it best to be a loyal partner and have a stable relationship for life?* Every relationship she'd enjoyed had been the kind of 'open' type that Norma despised. Her sister had been too frightened to dive into any partnership at all. Deep down in the core of her being, Bernie knew why, and why she herself had been promiscuous since the age of sixteen. She also had a good idea why her mother had never remarried. To admit it to Norma would be like baring her soul a little too much. Bernie pulled her coat around her against the cool evening air, and walked a little faster.

# Chapter Forty – Norma
## 2015

Norma smiled and sat down in a chair opposite Susan Meredith.

"Hello."

"My, my…" Susan Meredith looked at Norma in surprise. "How you've changed in just one year!"

Norma chuckled.

"I've lost four and a half stones and I've also now got a job. All the exercise I do as a hospital porter helps to keep the weight down and makes me fit. I don't need to take Metformin any more, and I've even made a friend."

"I'm so happy for you, Norma. I can see you're coping extremely well as a woman. Have you encountered any problems along the way?"

"Yes, my family. It took some of them a long while to accept the new me."

Doctor Meredith nodded.

"Yes, that often happens, I'm afraid. Some people, especially older ones, don't like change. Anything else?"

Norma crossed one leg over the other and sat back in her chair.

"Erm… yes… I feel absolutely more at home in my own skin, but please… would it now be possible for me to be put on the waiting list for surgery? You see, if I ever *do* get around to having a sexual relationship, I can only do this as a woman and with another woman. I can't really see it happening anyway, but nevertheless I just can't cope anymore with having male genitalia, now everything's going so well."

Doctor Meredith jotted down a few notes and then looked up at Norma.

"I totally understand. Yes, I think I shall now refer you to Mister Eric Balaam, the surgeon who can do your gender reassignment operation at Saint Mark and Saint Matthew's Hospital. I'll call it the *MMH* for short. He'll call you in for a clinic appointment beforehand just to satisfy himself that you still want to go ahead with it. There'll be a bit of a waiting list, maybe about six to eight months, but rest assured you'll be on his list."

"Thanks so much." Norma let out a sigh of relief. "You don't know what this means to me. *And* I'm rather glad that it won't be at the hospital where I work."

"No, they only do that kind of surgery at the *MMH*. Anything else I can help you with?" Doctor Meredith asked.

Norma shook her head.

"No thanks. I think you've done more than enough. I'm very grateful."

Doctor Meredith stood up and extended her right hand.

"You won't need to come back and see me anymore. The next person you'll see will be Mister Balaam. Good luck, Norma."

Norma shook Susan Meredith's hand.

"Thank you. You don't know what this means to me."

\*\*\*

Norma clinked her glass against Bernie's.

"I'm on the list for surgery... woo hoo!"

"Fantastic!" Bernie exclaimed. "That's really good news!"

Norma sipped some lemonade, and then to her surprise felt Bernie's lips on hers.

"A celebratory kiss. Nothing else. Well done, Norma."

From her peripheral vision she noticed Jack, who had raised an upturned fist in her direction. A river of emotions ran through her head at the thought of somebody right at that moment had chosen to be in her personal space.

"Nobody's ever kissed me before, maybe apart from my mum back in the dark ages." Norma looked into Bernie's eyes and smiled. "I can't believe you just did that."

Bernie shrugged.

"As I said, it's nothing. If anyone deserves a kiss... you do."

Norma touched Bernie's arm in silent thanks. From his vantage point behind the bar, Jack sent her an obscene gesture and blew a kiss of his own. At that precise moment she yearned for nothing else but the courage to return Bernie's act of kindness. Instead, she wiped her eyes and let out a hoot of shaky laughter.

"I'm a late developer, as you can see. I learned a word from Jack a while back... *asexual*. I've always seen myself as asexual, I suppose."

"Nobody's asexual." Bernie shook her head. "Look at me... I've had more partners than I care to remember. Belinda had none, just like you, but that doesn't mean she was asexual. If I'm honest with myself I think I know why she chose not to get involved with anybody romantically, but it's a bit painful for me to talk about just at the moment."

Norma, unsure of what to say next, blurted out the first thing that came into her head.

"We all have secrets we'd rather keep hidden. Look at me... pushing sixty and only now I've had the courage to live true to myself. All I can say is that since I've brought everything out into the open I've never been happier. If you ever want to talk about it, then I'm here to listen."

"Thank you." Bernie downed a large vodka and tonic in one go. "One day I might, but at the moment I think you've enough to get on with. You don't need to deal with all my dirty laundry as well."

Norma opened a bag of crisps and held it out to Bernie.

"Cheers." Bernie took a crisp off the top. "We're getting a bit maudlin here. I think I need another vodka."

# Chapter Forty One - Bernie

Bernie laid on her bed in the room she had shared with her sister as a child. Downstairs she could hear her mother's voice rise and fall as she talked on the telephone. Outside the open window birds twittered in the late afternoon heat, a neighbour's dog barked, and somewhere nearby a baby screamed for attention.

*Why had nobody rescued her when she had screamed? Had it really been over forty years ago?*

She looked across to Belinda's bed, still with its pink duvet and pillowcase as though the occupant would soon be returning to sleep the slumber of the righteous.

*How many nights had she cuddled that little five year old girl, knowing full well the reason for her tears?*

The tinkling laughter from downstairs grated on Bernie's nerves. Her mother was altogether too happy for somebody who had done nothing to stop the almost nightly abuse her two young daughters had suffered at the hands of their father.

Bernie needed to get away. Her mother's desire for support and companionship had started to grate on her nerves. However, the idea of going home to Mark did not cause her heart to beat faster in the excited anticipatory way that it used to. She was at a crossroads in her life; tired of drinking to ease the pain, and weary of one night stands with faceless people who cared nothing for her and instead just for a moment wished to escape their own depressing realities.

*What had she achieved in her fifty one years? What had she to show for five decades of life?* Bernie lit a cigarette and watched smoke curl to the ceiling. Her father's heart attack had finally put a stop to the anguish that her, her mother and Belinda had suffered, but the legacy of his abuse had gone on to affect every aspect of their future lives. None were able to give their trust to anybody, and she knew that Belinda, just like her, had fought her own demons.

She stubbed the cigarette out in an ashtray, and stood up. It was time to face her troubles head on.

\*\*\*

Her mother ended the call and turned around to face her.

"That was your auntie Sal. She sends her love."

Bernie flopped down in an armchair.

"It's a good job somebody does, then."

"What's that supposed to mean?" Sonia Smithson, annoyed, looked at Bernie. "Just because I'm not a demonstrative person, it doesn't change the fact that I've always loved you and your sister."

"You already *know* what I mean." Bernie locked eyes with her mother. "So don't come the old innocent with me. *You* know why Belinda killed herself just as well as *I* do."

A pause lengthened into minutes as Bernie's gaze remained fixed on her mother. Sonia was the first one to break the silence.

"I've dreaded this for years, because I knew and this conversation would eventually come up. Yes, I *do* know why, but like you, I decided it was perhaps best to keep everything hidden. No good will come of raking up old wounds from the past."

"Why didn't you stop it?" Bernie hissed. "Why did you let him carry on doing what he did to us? We both told you what was going on, and yet you did nothing."

Bernie's eyes glittered. She watched her mother start to pace the room. Sonia reached the bay window, glanced into the street, and then very slowly turned around.

"Who says I didn't stop it?" She answered in a whisper. "I *did* stop it in the only way I knew how to."

Bernie sat up straighter.

"How?"

She could see a streak of tears had run down her mother's cheeks. Sonia wiped her eyes and sighed.

"I was terrified of him, and for your information he abused me too, but we won't go there. Anyway...back in the days when family doctors prescribed medications for six months at a time, I took note of how that terribly thin singer, Karen somebody or other, with anorexia had died; she had taken thyroxine when she didn't need it to speed up her metabolism, and it had given her a fatal heart attack. Dad was on thyroxine because he'd had his thyroid out as a teenager, and he'd always left it to me to put his medications out at meal times. I remember there were three different thyroxine tablets giving three different doses. I just gave him three of the highest doses every day over a period of a several months. I told him to order another supply before we went on holiday, and so he did. He would never go and see a doctor, and he only ever had one blood test a year. He complained that he felt hot and had a fast heartbeat, but he didn't realise what caused it. I did it for you two, because he was a big, strong man, and I wasn't brave enough to whack him over the head when he was asleep."

Stupefied, Bernie sat open-mouthed and stared at her mother.

"Why did you never say anything? He's been gone for so many years."

Sonia shrugged.

"The deed was done, and it was enough that he was no longer around. I couldn't turn back time and take your unhappiness away or take back the abuse we had all suffered. Also I could never trust another man, especially with you two around, and so I never remarried. I just swept it all under the carpet and tried to make the rest of your childhood happy. So hey…don't say that I've never loved you, because that simply isn't true."

Bernie, tearful, stood up and then silently ran over to her mother and gave her a hug.

## Chapter Forty Two - Norma

It was quite obvious to Norma that Bernie had something on her mind. She had lost her *joie de vivre*. Her friend had been unusually quiet all evening, and had taken scant notice of the live band who now packed away their instruments. Jack rang the bell for last orders, and Norma took out her purse.

"Want another drink before we go?"

"Ah, no. It's okay."

Norma, afraid that Bernie had grown tired of her company, stood up and grabbed her bag.

"I'll walk back home now, so… see you at the weekend if you like?"

"Sure. Sorry I've been a bit quiet tonight."

"Is anything wrong?" Norma asked with some trepidation. "Have I said or done anything to upset you?"

Bernie shook her head.

"No, it's not you. I need to make some changes in my life. I envy you in a way… you've got all your shit sorted out now, and I've only just started."

"It took me fifty seven years though." Norma chuckled. "If you need any help, then let me know."

"Don't go just yet… I think I will have another drink, but just a coke."

"Okay." Norma looked over at Jack behind the bar. "Two cokes please."

Jack raised his right thumb.

"You two ladies are really pushing the boat out tonight."

"Payday isn't until Friday." Norma laughed. "I'm skint. Every night I'm in here and give you all my money."

"Have 'em on me, babes." Jack slid two cokes along the bar. "You've got another half an hour."

\*\*\*

The silence had become embarrassing. Norma downed her coke in record time and stood up.

"Sorry, I think it's time for me to go."

Bernie nodded and finished her drink.

"Can I walk back some of the way with you?"

"Sure." Norma gathered her things together. "Whatever you like."

They had traversed most of Fulham High Street before Bernie spoke.

"My mum told me that she killed my father. I can't get my head around it."

Norma wondered if she had heard right. She stopped in her tracks and looked at Bernie.

"Pardon?"

"Yeah, you heard." Bernie shrugged. "Mum couldn't take it anymore and did him in. I won't go to the police or anything like that, because if *she* hadn't done it then *I* would have as soon as I'd figured out a way."

The urge to say something… anything…caused Norma to blurt out the first words that came into her head.

"How? Ah… how did she do it?"

"Overdosed the bastard on thyroxine but he didn't know it." Bernie gave a hollow laugh. "The bloke ran about like a headless chicken for months before his heart exploded."

"I'm so sorry." Norma placed an arm on Bernie's shoulder. "Did he abuse her?"

Bernie nodded.

"Her, me, *and* Belinda. We all suffered night after night. *I'm* not sorry. He deserved all he got."

As they approached Crozier Road and the parting of the ways, Norma gave Bernie a quick hug.

"Come in and have a coffee before you go back. Mum will be asleep, so we can sit in the kitchen if you like so as not to wake her up."

"Have you got any whisky to put in it?" Bernie asked with the hint of a smile. "No, on the other hand, just the coffee please. I'll try and turn over a new leaf."

"Mum only likes sherry."

"Yuck." Bernie pulled a face. "You can keep that."

When they reached number 36, Norma undid the gate as quietly as she could and closed it behind Bernie. Her mother had left the outside light on, and the porch door was unlocked. Norma turned her key in the lock and opened the main front door.

"Follow me into the kitchen and I'll put the kettle on."

The fluorescent light spluttered into life and illuminated the kitchen. Norma closed the door behind them, switched the kettle on to boil, and took a tin of biscuits out of the cupboard.

"I'm not supposed to eat these, but hey, they go well with coffee."

"It's only now after fifty odd years that I've decided to look after myself." Bernie took a biscuit and sat down at the breakfast bar. "I've done everything to excess to try and drown out what he did to me, but it hasn't worked. Belinda obviously had issues, but she kept to herself. I always thought she was over it, but now I'm sure I know too well why she did what she did."

Norma, adrift on an uncommon sea of emotion, took comfort in the practicalities of making coffee. She placed a hot cup in front of her friend and sat beside her.

"I can't even begin to imagine what you're going through. My dad died when I was fourteen, but cancer got *him*."

"We were all dependent on Dad." Bernie sighed. "He wouldn't let her work, but Mum would never have left... he would have killed her and she knew it. She blossomed after he died. She got a job and learned to drive. Hey, I don't want to talk about that prat any more. Let's talk about something else."

They munched their way through half a packet of biscuits before Norma spoke.

"I haven't known you long, but you're the best friend I've never had."

Bernie chuckled.

"With friends like me, who needs enemies?"

Norma sipped her coffee, moved her stool nearer to Bernie's, and then did the hardest thing she had ever done. She put an arm around Bernie's shoulders and gave her a hug.

"*I* needed a friend like you, and there you were. Like magic."

Bernie leaned into Norma and closed her eyes.

"I can't face going back to Mum tonight. Can I crash on your settee? I'll be long gone before your mum wakes up in the morning... promise."

Norma did not want the moment to end. Her senses were heightened with the aroma of Bernie's perfume and the feel of her friend's body next to hers. She tried to ignore the hated erection, and cursed the day she had been born male.

"Of course. I'll get you a duvet and some spare pillows."

With reluctance she disentangled herself and crept along the passageway to the airing cupboard. With two pillows and a duvet under her arm, Norma went into the front room where Bernie had already made herself at home on the settee.

"Hope you sleep okay."

She was surprised when Bernie stood up and kissed her full on the mouth.

"I'm sure I will."

The opportunity she had waited so long for was about to pass her by. Norma despised herself, but the timing was wrong.

"Night night. See you in the morning."

***

Sleep eluded her with the certainty of Bernie so near, and yet light years away. Norma, glad of her late shift the following day, tossed, turned and twisted the sheets into a knot. Around 03:00 she sat up, alarmed, at the sound of a faint tap on her bedroom door. Bald, naked, and totally vulnerable, she froze rigid with fear in her bed as the door creaked open.

"Norma!" Bernie hissed. "Are you awake?"

Mouth dry with nerves, Norma remained silent. She peeped through her lashes and saw the naked form of Bernie as she flitted across the bedroom floor towards the bed. Norma's heart turned somersaults in her chest.

"What do you want?" Norma whispered. "I haven't got any clothes on!"

Bernie hopped into bed beside her.

"Neither have I. I just want a cuddle."

A warm arm came across Norma's abdomen, and a heavy leg draped over her thighs. Bernie's head lay on her shoulder, and Norma, no longer wracked with fear, put one arm around Bernie's shoulder and decided the experience was altogether extremely pleasant. Another pulsing erection grew under the bedclothes.

"I'm sorry about my body."

Bernie yawned.

"Shut up and go to sleep."

## Chapter Forty Three - Agnes

Her knees creaked, and her fingers were so stiff that it was difficult to grip the trolley. Agnes shook her hands about in the air, marched on the spot, and then had another go. On the second attempt she was able to push the trolley forward and escape the confines of her bedroom.

She entered the kitchen and to her annoyance saw that the light had been left on all night. The remains of a packet of biscuits littered the breakfast bar, along with two unwashed cups which contained congealed dregs of milky coffee.

*Two* cups? Agnes wracked her brain but could not remember drinking any coffee the night before, and she certainly would have remembered if she had eaten so many biscuits. She picked up the cups, put them on her trolley, and wheeled them over to the sink. She filled a bowl full of hot soapy water and put the cups in to soak, then trundled over to the breakfast bar again with a wet cloth to wipe down the surface.

With the kitchen back to how she liked it, it was time to make Norman a cup of tea. She pushed her trolley over to the fridge, took out a pint of milk, and put the milk on top of the trolley. After she had taken two clean cups from the cupboard she switched the kettle on to boil.

Pot warmed and tea made, she leaned against a bar stool, downed half her tea in one go, and then put Norman's full cup and saucer on top of her trolley. On her way past the front room she looked in and was surprised to find two pillows and a duvet minus its cover on the settee. Agnes was not sure what had been going on, but was determined to talk to Norman about it.

The cup rattled in its saucer as Agnes made her way along the passage to Norman's room. To her surprise the door to his bedroom was slightly ajar. Agnes leaned forwards over the trolley and pushed the door open wide enough to get the trolley through.

"Norman... sorry ... Norma, I've made you some tea."

Agnes looked over at the bed and took a sharp intake of breath. An unfamiliar woman, half naked to the waist, lay asleep against her son's bare breasts. Norman, minus his wig and with a night's growth of beard, looked at her with red-faced embarrassment.

"Just leave it on the side, Mum. I'll drink it in a minute."

The sound of his voice woke the woman, who hastily covered her nakedness with a sheet.

"Morning Missus Wicks. I'm Bernie, Norma's friend."

Agnes closed her mouth, which had dropped open in surprise.

"Yes, I'm sure you are, my dear."

She backed the trolley out as fast as her aged legs would carry her. As she stepped out into the passage and closed the door she heard a burst of suppressed giggling erupt from inside the room. Heavy-footed, she trudged along to the front room, a gooseberry in her own home, and so very, very old.

\*\*\*

*What should she do? Should she make the woman a cup of tea or leave them alone?* Agnes decided on the latter, and instead put a few rashers of bacon in the microwave. By the time she almost finished her sandwich, the woman, now fully clothed, came into the kitchen.

"Sorry about the shock you had, Missus Wicks. Norma helped me out last night when I needed a friend."

*Yeah, I bet he did.*

"He's kind like that." Agnes blurted out the first words that came into her head. "He'll do anything for anyone."

The woman stood in front of her and looked with hungry eyes at the plate which still contained a sliver of sandwich. Agnes, unwilling to offer Norman's rashers to the woman, ignored her stares.

"Would you like a cup of tea?"

"Oh, yes please. Don't get up, I'll make it. I don't bother with a teapot. Just a tea bag in a cup is okay for me."

Agnes' face registered a faint displeasure.

"Whatever you like."

She looked at Norman, who entered the kitchen in his best ginger wig and a bright pink housecoat.

"There's some bacon in the fridge for you, Norman."

"Oh, I'm not hungry. Bernie can have it."

"*Great.*" Bernie gave a thumbs up sign. "Got any oil, Missus Wicks?"

"No." Agnes shook her head. "I always put my bacon in the microwave."

She saw the woman grimace.

"Ooh-er, never tried that. Okay, whatever… I'll always try anything once."

*Yeah, I bet you would…*

Agnes did not like the woman; she had made herself too much at home already. Little by little she knew the woman would chip away at her son's allegiance to his mother until the last vestige had been eradicated. *How long would it be before the pair of them shoved her into one of those godawful residential homes to get her out of the way?* Agnes shuddered, as though somebody had walked over her grave.

\*\*\*

At last Ruth had cottoned on to the fact that she liked to watch the end of *Pointless*. However, when the phone rang at 6pm on the dot, Agnes picked it up and sighed.

"Oh, I almost sat down to watch the Six O'clock News then."

She heard a *tut* of irritation at the other end.

"*Mother*, there never seems to be *any* good time to give you a call, does there?"

"Six thirty would be better, Ruth. Anyway, how are you?"

"I'm fine. How's it with you?"

"Norman's got a *girlfriend*." Agnes stated with relish. "She was in his bed this morning when I went in with his cup of tea."

"In his *bed*? Good God!" Ruth chirruped. "Who the hell would fancy *him*?"

Agnes chuckled.

"*She* obviously does. They were both naked as the day they were born, but then he got up and came in the kitchen with his wig and pink dressing gown on. He gave her his bacon as well."

"What's her name?" Ruth asked with interest.

"Bernie."

"Is that short for Bernard? Is she a man?"

"No." Agnes laughed. "Definitely a woman."

"Well, I'll go to the foot of our stairs."

Agnes felt momentarily powerful and the fount of all knowledge. For the first time in ages she took her eyes off the TV and enjoyed the fact that finally there was some important news of her own to impart to her daughter.

"Apparently she'll stay overnight tomorrow as well. The pair of them seem to have clicked."

"I'll be round tomorrow evening." Ruth stated firmly. "I have to see all this for myself."

## Chapter Forty Four - Ruth

She could not wait to get off the phone to the old girl and inform June and Steven what their mother had said. Ruth replaced the receiver, then picked it up and tapped in June's number.

"Will you be on that phone all bloody night?" Gordon complained. "What's the scandal, then?"

"Tell you in a minute."

With some dismay she heard the engaged tone. She flung down the receiver.

"Out with it then." Gordon put the TV on mute. "Something's happened. What?"

Ruth paused after picking up the receiver for a third time.

"Mum found Norman in bed with a woman this morning."

"Christ!" Gordon guffawed. "It's about bloody time!"

"The woman's called Bernie, and they were both naked."

Gordon appeared confused.

"Bernie? Is it a bloke?"

"No, apparently not. Can you believe it? I'm trying to phone June, but I expect Mum's already told her about it. I'll phone Steven instead."

She heard her brother's phone ring out loud and clear.

"Hello?" Ruth suffered a frisson of disappointment on hearing her sister-in-law's voice.

"Hi Hannah, it's Ruth. Is Steven there?"

She heard Hannah shout up the stairs, but could not make out the faint reply.

"Sorry Ruth, he's in the shower. Can I take a message?"

"Oh, er... just that Mum found Norman naked in bed with a woman this morning."

Her sister-in-law's response after a brief silence was not the reply she expected.

"I expect that's *his* business, isn't it? He's never phoned to let me know that *you're* in bed with Gordon."

Ruth, momentarily stunned into silence, could only manage a snort of laughter and then slammed the phone down.

"Bloody hell! No wonder Mum doesn't like her!"

"Gordon flipped through TV channels with the remote control.

What's she done *now*?"

"That's the last time I talk to *her* on the phone." Ruth, irate and somewhat deflated, flopped back onto the settee. "She always *was* on his side."

She lifted the receiver and tapped in her sister's number once more.

"Is that you, Ruth?"

"Yeah." Ruth drummed her fingers on the arm of the settee. "Have I got some news for *you*."

June chuckled.

"I already know. Mum just told me. Well, well, I never knew he had it in him. It must have been a bit of a shock for the old girl."

"She's a tough old bird." Ruth replied. "It'd take more than *that* to upset her apple cart."

"It makes you wish you'd been there, doesn't it?"

Ruth let out a snort of disgust.

"Ugh! No, the last thing I'd want to do is see Norman naked."

"He's Norma now. We've got to call him Norma."

"Oh yeah. "Ruth gave a click of annoyance with her tongue. "So we have."

\*\*\*

Ruth noticed her brother's curtains were drawn when she walked up the garden path towards the front door of the bungalow the next evening. She rang the bell and waited. Curtains twitched in the bay window, and presently a stocky blonde woman in her late forties or early fifties came to the door.

"Who are you?" Ruth pushed past her into the house. "Have you kidnapped my brother?"

"Yeah. He's gone. You've got a sister instead."

Ruth turned around to face the woman, who laughed out loud.

"She's just getting dressed. We're going out for a drink. I'm Bernie, by the way."

"I'm Ruth. I've come to see my mother, actually."

"Agnes is in the kitchen."

Ruth nodded, uncertain of what to say next. She strode along the passageway, glad to escape the stranger's mocking eyes. In the kitchen her mother looked headless with her osteoporitic back bent over the sink.

"Hi Mum!" Ruth raised her voice. "Do you want me to do some washing up?"

She trundled the trolley a little nearer to Agnes, who gripped it and slowly turned around to face her.

"No thanks. Norma and Bernie made dinner tonight, so I'm washing up because I didn't help to cook it."

"You've got something to do that for you." Ruth pulled open the door of the dishwasher. "Load the crockery in *here*."

"No, I want to feel useful." Agnes shook her head. "I can do it."

Ruth stifled the urge to scream in frustration and picked up a tea towel.

"Norman cooked dinner? Good God! Is the old Queen dead?"

"She cooked chicken, chips and peas, with Bernie's help. Such nice girls."

Ruth applied the tea towel to a plate with more force than was necessary.

"He's not a girl, for Pete's sake!"

Her mother ignored the outburst. Instead, an answer emanated from the direction of the kitchen doorway.

"Yes, she is."

Ruth spun around to face Bernie, who regarded her with a steady gaze from two steely grey eyes.

"How *can* he be?" Ruth sighed and rolled her eyes. "He's got a dick in case you hadn't noticed."

"I *have* noticed." Bernie stated quietly. "But it's what's in her head that counts. The dick is only temporary."

As if on cue Ruth saw Norma appear behind Bernie, full breasts harnessed underneath a pale blue tunic top, and also wearing skinny jeans with kitten heeled boots. A shoulder-length ginger wig and full face make-up completed the ensemble. Ruth stood open mouthed in surprise at her brother's transformation.

"A *trans*-sister." She laughed. "Or is it a transistor? Jeez, why can't you have a fanny like everybody else?"

"Because I'm special." Norma shrugged. "Whatever. Get used to it. You've got three sisters now."

Agnes handed Ruth a wet saucepan.

"If *I* can do it, then so can *you*."

# Chapter Forty Five - Norma

Norma sniffed and wiped her eyes at the sight of her friend throwing the last of her possessions into a bulging suitcase.

"I'll miss you."

Bernie looked back over her shoulder.

"I told you… I've got to finish my relationship with Mark and sort my life out up north. I'll be back with a clean slate, hopefully in a couple of months or so, and then we can take up where we left off. I need to be down here for Mum too. I've avoided her for too long. Enjoy your new job, and I'll be here again before you know it."

Norma hurried over to Bernie and wrapped both arms around the best thing that had ever happened to her.

"Sorry to complain."

"Don't say *sorry*." Bernie returned the hug. "There's nothing to be sorry about."

"I'm on an afternoon shift today. I'll walk with you to the station."

Bernie smiled and disentangled herself.

"That'll be nice. I've got to get the tube to Earl's Court and then another one to King's Cross. Mark will pick me up at the other end."

"I'll tell Mum I'm going out, but come and have some breakfast first." Norma sighed. "You've got a long day ahead."

\*\*\*

A throng of people milled about outside Fulham Broadway station; their voices mingled with sounds made by the almost permanent stream of cars passing by. Norma, awkward and unsure what to say, grinned at Bernie.

"See you soon, eh?"

"Of course." Bernie put her suitcase down. "Give us a hug!"

The sensation of Bernie's body against hers was overwhelming. Norma closed her eyes and wished the moment could last forever.

"I haven't known you for very long, but I love you."

There. She had said it. The words had surprised her just as much as it had Bernie, who held herself at arm's length and looked into Norma's eyes.

"Nobody's ever said that to me before... not even Mark."

"I've never said it to anyone else either." Norma grinned and could not hide a rising excitement. "Not even to my family."

Bernie planted a kiss full on Norma's lips.

"You're a beautiful person, Norma. Be proud of who you are. Give me time and I'll be back. But now...I've got to go."

A river of tears threatened to cascade down Norma's cheeks as she watched her friend disappear through the station's glass doors. She had no idea how to present a happy face to the patients that afternoon at work.

\*\*\*

"Penny for them?"

Norma looked up from her cup of coffee at Jimmy's smiling face.

"Sorry. I just feel a bit low today."

Jimmy nodded.

"We all have those days, but as soon as I come to work and I wheel people to a ward or to x-ray, I realise there's so many worse off than me."

"You're right, I know." Norma sighed. "It's just that Bernie, a dear friend of mine, well… she's Belinda's sister actually, has had to leave to sort her life out. We got on so well, and now she's gone."

"I'm sure she'll be back. In fact I *know* she will. Something tells me there's much happiness in store for you."

Norma, surprised at her colleague's statement, stood up, suddenly buoyed.

"I hope so, Jimmy. I really hope so. Lord knows I could do with it."

"Come to my church tonight, there's a meeting on."

"Church?" Norma looked at Jimmy in confusion. "Oh, no. I'm not religious."

"It's a spiritualist church. We receive messages from the spirit world. In fact, your grandmother's stands right there behind you."

Norma jumped up and swung around in alarm.

"Don't say things like that. It gives me the creeps!"

"It's true. She says the day you came out was the best day of her life."

"But she's dead!" Norma took a second look at the empty space behind her. "Anyway... how did you know that about me?"

"I didn't. Your nan just told me."

Norma grimaced.

"Sorry. This is a bit too weird for me. I'd best get back to work."

"Me too." Jimmy stood up. "The Church of the London Spiritualists, Moorecroft Street. Eight o'clock. There's an awesome medium there tonight, Rae Cordelle. Don't forget."

Norma shook her head.

"Sorry. I'm not into all that."

"I am." Jimmy replied with a shrug. "It'll do you the world of good. Believe me."

## Chapter Forty Six - Norma

Promptly at eight o'clock Norma slid into a seat at the back of the church, a modern building quite unlike any church she had ever seen before. Nervous and afraid at what the evening might bring, she listened to the buzz of anticipation all around her, and when she felt a tap on her shoulder she nearly jumped out of her chair. With some relief she turned round to find Jimmy smiling at her.

"Glad you could come."

"I almost didn't." Norma signaled to Jimmy to sit down. "But hey, you got me interested."

"Hang on and enjoy the ride."

Jimmy took a seat beside her.

"We don't get Missus Cordelle here very often. She's much in demand, believe me."

A few minutes later an elderly man whom Norma took as a lay preacher climbed up the few steps to the stage, recited the Lord's Prayer along with the rest of the audience, and then spoke into a microphone.

"Good evening, ladies and gentlemen. Tonight I'd like to welcome the most accurate medium I've ever seen to our humble hall. Please give a round of applause to… Missus Rae Cordelle!"

A plump, middle aged woman with her black hair fashioned into a sleek bob stood up from a chair on the front row and took her place next to the preacher amidst enthusiastic applause.

"Hello everyone. Has anybody seen me work before?"

Norma saw a few hands shoot up. The medium gazed around the hall and then carried on.

"Well, for the others here who haven't attended a demonstration of clairvoyance before, don't worry. If you see anything scary I'll be the first one out of the door ahead of you all!"

Norma laughed and looked at Jimmy.

"I like her." She whispered. "Thanks for inviting me."

"She always says that. It breaks the ice a bit."

Norma focused her attention on the medium, who paced back and forth across the stage and did not take her eyes off the audience.

"Whatever you hear tonight, it's all due to my Red Indian spirit guide, Medicine Horse, who is the bridge between myself and the spirit world. Without his help I would not be able to impart messages at all from your loved ones. I also work with the police to help find people that have disappeared. Did you ever read about the missing boy, David Nelson, in the news? Well, David himself via Medicine Horse was able to tell me where his bones were."

There was a slight pause. A blanket of silence fell over the audience. Norma, uncertain as to what would happen next, watched Rae Cordelle momentarily close her eyes and then point at a young man who sat slightly in front of her on the opposite side of the hall.

"I'd like to come to the man wearing a light blue jacket. Just say yes or no to my statements if you like. I'll also stop if you want me to."

The man, obviously nervous, sat up straighter. His voice came out as a squeak.

"Yes?"

"I have your mother here. She says you mustn't grieve anymore. She is happy and free from pain."

Norma, alarmed, instantly saw the effect of the medium's words on the young man, who took a deep breath and then wiped his eyes with the back of one hand.

"Yes."

His voice came out as a whisper. Rae Cordelle continued to walk around the stage.

"She says she loves your new partner, and that she knows you'll be very well suited. Did you notice that your photo of her on the wall was crooked the other day?"

"Yes!" The man nodded in agreement. "I did!"

Rae smiled.

"That was her. She saw you move it back into place."

As a tide of emotion threatened to overwhelm the man, Rae tactfully walked to the other side of the hall.

"I'll say God bless. Can I come to the lady right at the back who is sitting with the gentleman, please?"

Norma looked from left to right but then noticed how the medium stared straight at her.

"Yes?" She cleared her throat. "You want *me*?"

"I do indeed." Rae nodded. "I have a lady here with me who has recently passed over. She has blonde hair and is around forty five to fifty years of age."

Suddenly nauseous, Norma's heart thumped in double time.

"Yes, I know who she is."

"She says she's sorry that she did what she did."

Norma tried to ignore the flush creeping over her and wondered if she might faint. Beside her, Jimmy patted her hand as she blurted out the first two words she could think of.

"Thank you."

Rae Cordelle gave a nod of acknowledgment.

"She says that she could only see one way out of her troubles, and that was the way she took. She tells you that somebody very dear to her loves you, but this person is not able to show any love because of what happened to her in the past."

"Yes."

Norma, her voice barely audible, stared at the medium and sensed the full force of the audience's stares.

"She's fading now, but she also says that the two of you will be very happy together. Do you understand what I say?"

Norma pulled out a tissue to wipe her eyes.

"I do."

"God bless you." Rae Cordelle paced to the opposite side of the stage. "Can I come to the man with the black, curly hair please?"

The audience turned their gaze away from Norma in an instant, and instead looked towards the direction the medium pointed. Norma, shell-shocked, stared at Jimmy.

"I can hardly believe what's happened. I can't wait to tell Bernie."

"I told you she was good, didn't I?" Jimmy chuckled. "You'll have to come again when she's here. Bring Bernie."

"I will." Norma nodded. "Definitely."

\*\*\*

"Bernie?"

"Yeah, hello Norma."

It was good to hear her voice. Norma gripped the phone and wondered how the hell to tell Bernie that her sister's spirit was still alive.

"Is it a bad time? I wondered how you're getting on."

"Oh… Mark's away for a few days, but I've started to try and close my life up here. I'll tell him about the split when he comes back rather than by a text message. It's not a good way to do it. How are you?"

"I'm fine, but I must tell you about a spiritualist church I went to tonight. I know it sounds weird, but Belinda came through via a fantastic medium, Rae Cordelle. Have you heard of her?"

"No. I don't go in for all that stuff."

"Neither do I usually, but Jimmy at work invited me. Bernie, I *know* it was Belinda. She said she was sorry for what she did, but she couldn't see any other way to solve her problems. It was an amazing night."

"Well, a lot of people *do* go in for that sort of thing, but it doesn't do much for me." Bernie cleared her throat. "If it helps to get *you* through the night though, then it's all good I suppose."

Norma closed her eyes and took a deep breath.

"Belinda said that you love me."

She hated the silence that followed, and fervently wished that she could turn back the clock.

"Did she? Well... if she says so then it must be true."

Norma sighed.

"You don't believe any of this, do you? Look, I've got to go now. It's late and I've got an early shift tomorrow. Hope to see you soon."

She ended the call and switched the phone off before Bernie had a chance to reply.

\*\*\*

Seven messages queued up to be read when Norma switched her phone back on again the following morning. Bernie had spent a sleepless night as well. Norma zipped through the first six '*call me/text me/*' messages until she came to the last one.

'*Yes I love you. If you switch your bloody phone on then I'll be able to tell you myself.*'

Norma looked at the clock – 05:45 and an hour and a half left to get to work. She tapped on Bernie's number, decided it was worth the risk of a bollocking, and pressed the 'call' button. A sleepy voice answered after several rings.

"What?"

"I've switched my bloody phone on."

She heard a throaty chuckle at the other end.

"And I *love* you. Sorry I'm such a prat. Can I go back to sleep now?"

"Yeah of course. I love you too. Bye bye."

"Piss off."

She could not keep the grin from her face.

## Chapter Forty Seven - Agnes

Something was coming her way, and she wasn't sure whether she would like it or not. Agnes looked at the two of them as they sat together on the settee and hoped they were not going to take over her house and put her in that residential home she had dreaded for so long.

"So... what do you say if Bernie comes to live here with us until we can get our own place?"

Agnes wondered if it was worth saying anything at all. The two of them had most likely already made up their minds. She wondered if her son had become so overwhelmed with the sudden explosion of his sex life that he would agree to go to bed with *anyone*.

But was he her *son* anymore? Granted, as far as she knew he still had male genitalia and looked outwardly more masculine than feminine, but there was a girlish side to him that had more recently come to the fore. She couldn't really say she had another daughter either, but at the end of the day did it matter a jot? Norma was happy in his/her world, and had at last found a girlfriend.

"And we'll help out with the cooking and housework." Norma looked at Bernie, who nodded. "We don't want you running around after us."

Agnes weighed up her options. If she said no, then she would be left on her own in a house that had become too much for her to cope with. If she let them stay, then she would have company on tap and someone on hand to share the burden of domestic duties. Who knew how much time she had left? They might even make her last years on earth more comfortable.

She looked from one to the other.

"You don't have to find a flat. You can stay here. I don't mind at all. Bernie, please call me Agnes. Missus Wicks sounds a bit too formal."

She smiled as she saw them visibly relax. When Bernie stood up to give her a kiss on the cheek, Agnes could not hide her surprise.

"Thanks very much, Agnes. And don't worry about the financial side of it, I'll soon get a few job interviews lined up. I've got some savings to use until I get a job, so I can help out with the shopping and bills."

"Thank you." Agnes touched her cheek. "You're welcome, I'm sure."

She watched the two of them walk arm-in-arm down the passage together towards their bedroom. They were the oddest couple she had ever seen. Agnes closed her eyes and sighed. *Whatever had happened to her son? How could she even think about controlling a grown man? Who was she to dictate how her son should live his life? What the hell… if he was happier to live as a woman, then so be it.* Agnes smiled. She now had three daughters instead of two.

\*\*\*

Unusual sounds penetrated her ears; somebody was actually up before *her*. A kettle came to the boil, cups rattled in saucers, and giggles emanated from the kitchen. Agnes sat up in bed at the sound of a knock on her bedroom door.

"Yes?"

Bernie, clad in sensible pajamas, entered the room and carried a full tray which contained a teapot, cup, saucer and spoon, and containers of milk and sugar. Norma, resplendent in a vivid pink nightdress and matching robe, held a packet of biscuits in one hand.

"We decided it was about time you had a cup of tea in bed, Mum."

Agnes, mouth wide open in disbelief, looked from one to the other.

"Thank you, Norma. To what do I owe this honour?"

"You've brought me enough cups of tea in bed over the years. It's payback time."

"Get used to it." Bernie laughed. "We have to be up early, but you don't. Enjoy it."

Agnes would rather have sat at the kitchen table to avoid biscuit crumbs in the bed, but instead decided to play along.

"This is *wonderful.*"

There was joy on their faces. Agnes bit into a biscuit. To quote her own mother, '*she had never known the like since old Leatherarse died*'.

## Chapter Forty Eight – Norma
## June 2016

On a blisteringly hot afternoon, Norma sat nervous and sweaty before Eric Balaam, a rather imposing middle aged man with silver hair. With features creased into a half smile he regarded her over the top of a pair of rimless spectacles.

"Miss Wicks, I have a referral here from Susan Meredith. This appointment is just to check that you still wish to go through with gender reassignment surgery."

"Oh *yes*." Norma nodded. "The sooner the better as far as I'm concerned."

"It's major surgery, as I expect you know, so I need to go over exactly what I'll be doing."

Norma chuckled.

"I've a fair idea."

"I will remove the testes and most of the penis, and the urethra will be cut shorter. I will then construct a vagina and vulva between the rectum and urethra from remaining parts of the penis. The erectile tissue will be used to create a clitoris. You will need to be prepared for severe pain, bruising and discomfort for some weeks afterwards. How long have you been living as a woman?"

"Oh, for some time now, around around eighteen months. I'm quite comfortable with it." Norma stated. "Even my family are getting used to it now."

"That's good." Eric Baalam tapped away at his keyboard. "Of course you will have a general anaesthetic and about a week's stay in hospital where we will give you pain relief and ensure that your kidneys are functioning properly as well. You will have to come in the day before the op and undergo tests, and we will also clear out your bowels so that you won't need to *go* for a few days. You will have a rod-shaped prosthesis inside your vagina for about five days afterwards. For around two months afterwards you will need to leave a dilator inside your vagina, but take it out to clean it every day. You will need to come back every week to be examined until I can see you have healed. Gradually you will be able to leave the dilator out for longer periods of time after the eight weeks, but if you do not use it then the vagina will be narrower and shorter than you might like."

Norma could see a light at the end of nearly sixty years of misery. She wanted to jump over the desk and give the surgeon a hug.

"When will it all take place?"

"The waiting list is about six months. So hopefully it will happen later this year. Until then, carry on living as a woman, and visit the counsellor again if you need it. Of course I will go through all the risks of this operation in more detail when you come in the day before, including bleeding, swelling, rupture of stitches, infection, scarring, and possible revision surgery. If you do change your mind, then I'd be grateful if you could let my secretary know.

"I won't need to do *that*." Norma shook her head slightly. "Thanks so much, and I look forward to the springtime."

"I will just need to examine you before you leave. Is that okay?"

"Oh... er... yes." Norma nodded.

"On rare occasions it may be possible to do away with the dilators, but for ninety eight percent of patients they are needed." Eric Balaam logged out and stood up. "On a different tack altogether, after about another six months you'll be able to apply for a Gender Recognition Certificate on the Government's website. You'll have to provide some ID documentation, but I'll be able to vouch for your transition if they need further proof."

"Wow, thanks for that info, Doctor Balaam. I didn't know about that."

\*\*\*

Norma stepped out of the main entrance of St. Mark and St. Matthew's Hospital and could have kicked herself for taking the easy option for so long. She waited at the bus stop and mused on all the years she had frittered away doing nothing when she could have built up a secretarial career or maybe even enjoyed a longer relationship with Bernie. She looked at the back of people's heads in front of her in the queue and wondered what life events they had suffered and triumphed over.

*Had she been given the shortest straw ever? Why had she done nothing and sat on her arse for so long? Why her? What had she ever done to have been born in the wrong body? As ever, she knew the answer was 'Why not?' and that the only person who could have made a difference all those years ago was herself.*

Norma sighed and wished that she was thirty years younger as she fished in her purse for the bus fare.

# Chapter Forty Nine – Norma
## November 2016

For a moment she did not know where she was. She had difficulty opening her eyes. Her mouth was parched and her lips dry. A disembodied voice floated by her right ear.

"You're in Recovery. The operation went very well."

"Water please." Norma squeaked. "Can I have some water?"

A hand which clutched a baby's beaker came into view.

"Just a sip. You're propped up. Drink a few drops. It's too soon to have much by mouth."

Water had never tasted so good. Norma managed a quick gulp and then tried to focus on the large clock on a wall in front of her. Five thirty. She wracked her brain to try and remember what the clock had read on the wall of the anaesthetic room. Had it been five past twelve? Had she really been in surgery for over five hours?

She fished about with one hand to lift the blanket covering her so that she could discover why her lower regions felt peculiar and unaccountably heavy. Her arm was gently placed back above the bedclothes.

"Plenty of time to do that later."

It was as though she could not wake up properly. Tubes for IV fluids, antibiotics and a morphine drip were connected to cannulas on the back of her hands. She had a blinding headache. Norma closed her eyes, and when she awoke it was three hours' later and she was back in a side room on the surgical ward and hungry; in fact hungrier than she had been in a long, long while.

A jug and a glass of water was on a wheeled bedside table in front of her. She pulled the table towards her and drank half the contents of the glass.

"Aha ...we've surfaced, have we?"

Norma looked up in confusion at a young healthcare assistant.

"Would you like some soup?"

"Does the Pope wear a dress?" Norma coughed. "Soup would be good, thanks."

In the privacy of her room she lifted the blanket and peered under her hospital gown to where a catheter was inserted. For the first time in her life her penis was not there. A momentary flash of alarm was followed by a rise of heady excitement. She was finally a woman!

"It'll look better than that in a few weeks' time."

Norma, embarrassed, replaced the covers in a flash. The night nurse held a welcome bowl of soup.

"Don't worry. They all do that. It's only natural to want to look."

Norma grinned.

"Thanks for the soup."

\*\*\*

Pain came in unremitting waves during the night. Patients on the ward outside moaned and shouted. Norma pressed the call button attached to her bed. A nurse appeared.

"Are you okay?"

"The pain is bad."

"You can alter the amount of the morphine drip. I'll show you."

Safe in the arms of Morpheus, Norma sunk into a doze, and just stirred briefly for an early-morning anti-coagulation injection. After breakfast and a bed bath she felt a little more human and asked a passing nurse for her wig and comb. After a fitful sleep, she opened her eyes to find the best remedy of all.

"Hi, sunshine. How's it going?"

Bernie sat on the chair beside her bed and popped grapes into her mouth from a plastic bag.

"Fucking awful. Are those grapes for me?"

"Yeah, but you were asleep."

Norma reached out to touch Bernie's hand.

"It's so good to see you. I'm in so much pain. I can't sit properly."

"Passionate sex is out then?" Bernie took another grape. "And there's me thinking my luck was in."

"Oh, don't make me laugh. Everything hurts."

She wanted to weep with the amount of discomfort she was in. Bernie's hand reached out to hold hers.

"Let it out. That's what I'm here for."

"If I start crying, I'll never stop." Norma shook her head and squeezed Bernie's hand. "I'm not sorry I had the op, it's just that I'm in so much pain I don't know what to do with myself."

"I take it you don't want to see Ruth then? She's outside."

"Oh God, not *Ruth*. *Just* who I want at my sick bed."

"Now she's retired she said to me she can visit you more often."

"You *are* joking, aren't you?"

She looked for a twinkle of laughter in Bernie's eyes, but there was none.

"Not at all. She's already bored at home with Gordon. She wants to prop up your pillows and check your catheter."

Norma craned her neck to see beyond the door, where Ruth appeared to give her the briefest wave.

"My day is complete."

"Have a word with her. I'll wait outside for a mo." Bernie stood up. "I think she wants to tell you something."

"Yeah, I bet she does." Norma sighed. "Send her in then."

The sight of her sister filled her full of dismay, who walked towards her and clutched a large bouquet of flowers.

"They're lovely." Norma replied without emotion. "Thanks."

Ruth put the flowers to one side and then picked up the clipboard at the end of the bed.

"What are you doing?" Norma tried to sit up straighter. "That's private."

"Whoops. Sorry. Old habits." Ruth clipped the board back to the bed. "Too many years of nursing. Anyway, Norma, how are you? I want to tell you I think you're very brave to have had this op. If there's anything I can do to help you, just say."

Norma hid her surprise.

"Thank you. Maybe come round to help Mum out until I'm back on my feet."

"Sure." Ruth nodded. "I didn't bring her today, but I *can* do tomorrow if you like. I'll get June to come in too. Steven's at work as usual, but he sends his love."

Norma laid back on the pillows and closed her eyes.

"Cheers, Ruth."

"I'll leave you with Bernie, but I'll see you again tomorrow. Just wanted to give you the flowers."

She kept her eyes closed until Bernie's hand slipped into hers.

"Can't believe my sister just turned up." Norma wiped her eyes. "Everyone's being so kind."

"You've gone through a lot. Just wait until you've recovered. She'll be all snarling and nasty again."

Norma grinned through her tears.

"I love you."

"I Love you too." Bernie kissed her cheek. "Till death us do part."

Pain could not dull her happiness. It might have taken her sixty years to grow up, but Norma decided then and there that she would never waste another moment.

"When I've recovered from this I'm going to have some surgery on my face so that I look more feminine. At last I've got something worthwhile to spend my dole money on."

"Norma, don't even think about more surgery at the moment. You've had enough for now."

Norma nodded.

"Yes I know, but it'll be the icing on the cake for me, so to speak. I won't rest until I've had it."

"I know you won't." Bernie replied. "But for now you've got to."

## Chapter Fifty – Norma
## September 2018

"I'm Miss Thurston, and I'm a craniofacial and plastic surgeon, but you can call me Sara. So you would like to have facial feminisation surgery?"

Norma looked across the desk to where a woman in late middle age sat and peered at her over rimless spectacles.

"Yes please. I've already had gender reassignment surgery, and this will be the last step."

"I understand." The surgeon nodded. "Patients can have surgery to reduce the size and shape of the forehead, alter and refine the nose, make the lips fuller and the cheeks rounder, decrease the chin's size and shape, and shave the Adam's apple. We can also do hair transplant surgery. It's up to you if you have just one or all of the procedures. Several of them can be done at once in an operation which lasts maybe six to ten hours, or you can have procedures spaced out. Of course to space them out would incur more cost. Would you know exactly which surgeries you would like?"

"Oh, as many as I can afford, for sure, and all at the same time to get them over with, apart from the hair transplant. I'm happy that I'm able to chop and change my wigs, and I don't think it worked for Elton John either. In for a penny, in for a pound. I've had forty years to save up, and so I'm ready to go."

Miss Thurston chuckled.

"It does give patients a greater sense of self-worth. I myself prefer to carry out upper face surgery and lower face surgery at different times. Of course each surgery will require a night's stay in hospital. You will suffer bruising and swelling, which will take about seven days to resolve and about a month for you to fully recover. The final result will not be evident until about a year after surgery, so you see, it will not be a quick fix."

"Hah, somebody else once said that." Norma sighed. "It seems nothing ever *is* for me."

"But you've come so far already."

"I waited too long for all this, Doctor. I wish I could have had this done in my twenties. But hey, I didn't have the money then. Going nowhere for forty years does have its advantages."

Norma reached out and took a thick file that the surgeon passed across the table.

"Have a look at these before and after pictures, and you will be able to see what a difference surgery makes. If you are agreeable, I can examine you, take some measurements, and we can make a plan to suit."

"*Wow.* Can you really make me look like these women?" Norma flipped through the pages. "This is wonderful work."

"Thank you. Yes of course I can. It's my specialty."

"What can I say?" Norma shrugged. "I can't wait. Please go ahead."

"Because feminine facial features are more petite than male facial features and because you are in your sixties, there may be excess laxity of the skin afterwards which might not resolve on its own. You may or may not require a further procedure in the form of a facelift, probably about six months after the last of the surgeries."

"*Great.*" Norma laughed. "I'll end up looking twenty years younger into the bargain. Doctor, nothing will put me off. I want the lot, and I want it *now!*"

\*\*\*

"Don't do it for *me*. I love you just as you are."

Norma looked up from her newspaper at Bernie in the chair opposite.

"I'm not doing it for *anyone*. I'm doing it to look more like a woman and feel better about myself."

"Just as long as you're sure." Bernie replied with a sigh. "You're absolutely fine as you are as far as I'm concerned."

"Thanks for your support." Norma gave Bernie a smile. "No more after this. I promise."

"You'll resemble Quasimodo for weeks afterwards."

Norma laughed.

"I already look like him now. You won't recognise me when Miss Thurston's finished. I'm not sure I'll even recognise myself."

"Well, there you go then. All the more reason for not going ahead with all that surgery."

"Stop worrying." Norma waggled a finger at Bernie. "You sound just like my old Mum."

Bernie looked wistful.

"I miss her."

"I do too, a bit." Norma folded up the newspaper and threw it across to Bernie. "But hey, she was old. She had a good life, and it was her time to go. She would have hated it that we sold the house, but at least everybody got their fair share of the money. It wouldn't have been right to stay there."

"We've started again. Just you and me."

Norma nodded.

"Scary isn't it? We've got to keep up with the rent or we'll get kicked out."

"Welcome to the real world, lover."

# Chapter Fifty One – Norma
## October 2019

She looked at Miss Thurston's two photographs that had been newly inserted at the back of her file, and shook her head in wonder. On the left a bald head, wide forehead, large hooked nose, cleft chin and thin lips. On the right she hardly recognized herself; plumper lips and cheeks, and smaller nose, chin, ears and forehead completed the transformation along with her favourite ginger wig.

"I can't believe this. Sara, what you've done is incredible. All that pain was worth it. When we visited my sister June recently after she had returned from a three month cruise, she was convinced Bernie had got herself a new girlfriend."

Sara Thurston chuckled.

"You've been through a lot. I must say, not many of my patients go the whole hog. The surgery has done wonders for your looks. I can see how happier you are by just looking at your expression."

Bernie nodded.

"I can't thank you enough. I shall shout out your name from the rooftops. I would like to have had the facelift, but I promised Bernie that I wouldn't have any more operations."

"There's not a lot of lax skin, but you know where I am if you ever change your mind."

Norma relaxed against the back of her chair.

"Sometimes I still can't believe I've got to the end of the road. I remember where I was just five years ago, and I shudder."

Sara Thurston typed a few notes into her computer.

"If you'd known back in two thousand and fourteen what you'd have to go through to become a woman, would you have stayed as Norman?"

"No, definitely not." Norma shook her head. "It was something I *had* to do."

Sara stood up and reached across the table with her right arm.

"Congratulations, Norma. You have my best wishes for the future."

Norma shook the outstretched hand and hoped the Grim Reaper would give her at least another twenty five years.

"Thank you. Thanks very much."

"My pleasure."

\*\*\*

There was a spring in her step as she strode along the pavement. Nobody sniggered or gave her a second glance, and that was fine as far as Norma was concerned. She was proud of her new trim figure, and vowed to eat as much healthy food as she could. She had been given a second chance at life, and it was time to grab it with both hands.

## Chapter Fifty Two – Norma
## April 2020

Norma turned off the bedside light and snuggled down beside Bernie.

"Just think… all those years I sat in my bedroom, and now bloody Covid's locked me up *again*."

Bernie chuckled.

"Ah, but now you've got *me*, you're the woman you always wanted to be, we've got our own place, and you've still got your job to go to, and so what are you complaining about?"

"I'm nearly at retirement age." Norma sighed. "All those places in the world I want to see before I peg it."

"And you will, if you're motivated enough." Bernie gave Norma a squeeze. "You haven't got one foot in the grave *yet*."

"I'm just impatient for it all to end. I never considered that I'd be living through a pandemic. It's something that happened in nineteen eighteen and the sixteen hundreds. It seems so… so *retro* somehow. Mum's been gone almost two years now. I could go anywhere in the world I like in theory, but then … *lockdown*."

She felt the weight of Bernie's head on her shoulder.

"The virus didn't target *you* specifically. It hasn't got it in for *you*. You haven't got the monopoly on misery."

"I know." Norma put an arm around Bernie. "I'm just sick of it already. I've got my life sorted, my face sorted, and now I've been kicked in the balls again."

"You haven't got any balls."

"Oh, figuratively speaking." Norma grinned. "Am I glad I got rid of *those*."

"We could plan somewhere to go on holiday when it's all over, if you like?"

Norma yawned.

"I've never been abroad. Mum never had the money to take four of us. I want to see it *all*. I want to make up for lost time."

"You want a lot, don't you?"

"I've wasted so many years. I could kick myself."

Bernie hoisted herself up on one elbow to look at Norma.

"Don't torture yourself with regrets. Look at me... Belinda killed herself and I had to live with the father from hell. Don't you think *I'm* angry too? I see loving parents and happy kids everywhere. Why *me*? Why did I have to go through all that shit?"

"Why not? Why should *you* be exempt?" Norma giggled. "How do *you* like it now the boot's on the other foot?"

Bernie flopped down beside her with a grin and draped one leg over Norma's thighs.

"Let's do something spectacular to mark the end of lockdown, whenever that may be. Shall we?"

Norma nodded.

"I've already thought about that. I'd like to sit on one of those Caribbean beaches. I think that would suit me very well."

"We could stay in one of those *Sandals* resorts which are advertised on TV." Bernie gave Norma a nudge with her elbow. "Do you know what else they do there?"

"Drain our bank accounts?" Norma offered. "Ruth and Gordon went to Saint Lucia and stayed at a Sandals resort. They liked it, I think. What? What else?"

There was a pause before Bernie replied in a soft voice. "They offer marriage services."

Norma swallowed hard before deciding to break the pregnant silence. Her voice came out as a croak.

"Do they?"

"Yeah, they do. Fancy getting hitched?"

Norma wondered if she had heard correctly. She sat up and looked down on Bernie.

"Have you just asked me to marry you?"

"Too bloody right, I did." Bernie giggled. "What say you?"

"But … I mean… surely holiday places like that are just for straight couples?"

"Bollocks!" Bernie shook her head. "They lifted the ban on same-sex marriages back in two thousand and four."

"I'd better grab you then before somebody else does."

"Is that a yes?"

"Yes...*yes!*" Norma laid back down and threw her arms around Bernie. "Ruth, Steve and June are not going to believe this!"

"They might even want to fly out and attend." Bernie suggested. "Anyway, give us a kiss to celebrate."

Norma grinned and planted a kiss on Bernie's lips.

"I can't wait for lockdown to end."

\*\*\*

Floor-length white chiffon framed each side of the canopy and floated around slightly in the hot July breeze. Norma took a quick glance over her shoulder, and there they all sat; June, Andrew, Steven, Hannah, Ruth, Gordon and Bernie's mother Sonia. Almost her entire immediate family apart from Billy, his wife and newborn daughter had turned up trumps for her wedding.

Waves crashed against the shoreline as holidaymakers, clad in bikinis and swimming trunks, strolled past three other couples in bridal attire who waited their turn outside the canopy. A steel band played calypsos on the sand. Norma, stifling hot in a long cream-coloured silk dress, turned towards the front again and squeezed Bernie's hand with her own.

"Have you had second thoughts?"

Bernie, wearing white shorts and a tee shirt, laughed to belie the fact that she was as nervous as hell.

"No. Have you?"

"Absolutely not!"

"Look at all the other couples waiting. This is like a conveyer belt."

Norma laughed.

"You could have worn something other than beach wear for our wedding."

"Well, we're on the beach, aren't we? I'm not the kind of girl who wears a dress."

"I am." Norma grinned. "Because I've worn trousers for most of my life."

The celebrant appeared with his assistant.

"Good afternoon ladies and gentlemen. Welcome to the marriage service of Norma Jane Wicks and Bernadette Ellen Smithson. I am Grant Harries, and am licensed as a celebrant to perform marriage services here in Saint Lucia. Would you all stand, please?"

Norma, heart beating a rapid tattoo, stood up as the celebrant came towards them.

"Norma and Bernadette do not feel the need to get married to demonstrate the inward love they feel for one another. You are not gathered here to witness what will be, but rather, what has already taken place in their lives. You are here to celebrate the outward commitment they wish to make to each other today in front of the people who mean the most to them. Norma and Bernadette. I call upon you both to make your vows to each other and to exchange rings."

Norma, with dread in her heart lest she forgot the words she had memorised so well, turned towards Bernie and took her hand.

"I, Norma Jane Wicks, promise to accompany you on life's adventure until death us do part. I promise to love, respect, listen to you and always try to understand you. I promise to allow you to be who you are and who you wish to be. You are the most loving person, so very kind and loyal. I will be ever thankful that you chose me to be your lifelong partner. Accept this ring as a symbol of my eternal love."

She placed a gold band engraved with hearts on the third finger of Bernie's left hand, and looked into her eyes.

"I love you."

Somebody blew their nose in the audience. She wished not for the first time, that her mother could have seen how happy she had become. She squeezed Bernie's fingers as her wife-to-be stated vows in a confident voice which rang out loud and clear.

"I, Bernadette Ellen Smithson, promise to remain loyal and faithful to you, Norma Jane Wicks, for the rest of my life. You deserve much happiness, and I intend to make you happy to the best of my ability. You are the most beautiful person inside and out, brave and loving. Thank you for agreeing to be my wife. I love you. Please accept this ring which is a symbol of my unending love."

Norma felt warmth on her wedding ring from Bernie's hot fingers. They stood side by side and held hands as the celebrant addressed them.

"Let your love comfort, support and encourage you. Let it be the best part of your lives. May you always know that love will make everything better and your world a place of happiness. I now pronounce that Norma and Bernadette are married to each other. There is a celebratory glass of champagne and wedding cake on the beach for everybody."

Norma heard loud applause behind her and took a quick look over her shoulder. There was not a dry eye to be seen. She leaned towards Bernie and stole a kiss, the first of many more to come in their new life together.

THE END

If you have enjoyed this book, please consider leaving a review. Thank you.

.

## OTHER BOOKS BY STEVIE TURNER

THE PILATES CLASS
A HOUSE WITHOUT WINDOWS
FOR THE SAKE OF A CHILD
LILY: A SHORT STORY
NO SEX PLEASE, I'M MENOPAUSAL!
A RATHER UNUSUAL ROMANCE
THE DAUGHTER-IN-LAW SYNDROME
REVENGE
THE NOISE EFFECT
CRUISING DANGER
THE DONOR
REPENT AT LEISURE
LIFE:  18 SHORT STORIES
ALYS IN HUNGERLAND
MIND GAMES
LEG-LESS AND CHALAZA
PARTNERS IN TIME
FINDING DAVID: A PARANORMAL SHORT STORY
EXAMINING KITCHEN CUPBOARDS
BARREN

Printed in Great Britain
by Amazon